THE ODDLYMPICS

ENJOY THESE OTHER ODD GOD ADVENTURES!

Odd Gods

The Oddyssey

ODD GODS

THE ODDLYMPICS

BY DAVID SLAVIN

ILLUSTRATED BY
ADAM J.B. LANE

BASED ON CHARACTERS BY
DAVID SLAVIN
AND DANIEL WEITZMAN

HARPER
An Imprint of HarperCollins*Publishers*

Library of Congress Control Number: 2020933705

ISBN 978-0-06-283957-2

Typography by Andrea Vandergrift

20 21 22 23 24   PC/LSCH   10 9 8 7 6 5 4 3 2 1

❖

First Edition

For my dad.
—D.S.

For Meredith, with thanks
—A.L.

I wonder what mud tastes like.

I mean, you see it all the time, right? Sometimes you step around it—and sometimes you step *in* it. Kinda gloppy, sorta chocolatey, even a little poopy-y. But what does mud *taste* like? And why, might you ask, would I wonder about something like that? Well, because I have a very strong feeling I'm about to find out.

It's the tug-of-war, the last event (thank Gods!) of our annual Mount Olympus Middle School color war, and my team is seconds away from getting creamed—or, I should say, *mudded*.

Our principal, Principal Deadipus, calls out, "Ready, Adonis?"

"The Gods were *born* ready!" roars my brother, the powerfully annoying Greek God Adonis. "Who wants mud pie?"

The rest of the Gods team—Poseidon, Aphrodite, and Heracles—chuckles along with him. So does the rest of our *entire school*. Then Principal Deadipus turns to me. "Ready, Oddonis?"

Yup, you heard him. I'm Oddonis. I'm an *Odd God*.

"Umm, I guess so," I answer weakly. The rest of the Odds team—Gaseous, Mathena, Puneous and Germes—gulps along with me.

"Coach Gluteus Maximus!" barks Deadipus to our gym teacher. "Begin!"

The coach blows his whistle, and we all start tugging. Then the strangest thing happens: nothing! We're pulling, they're pulling, but the rope's not moving! The Odds are actually even with the Gods. It's unbelievable!

"What the heck is going on here?" cries my

baffled brother to his teammates. "Aren't you guys tugging?"

"I'm tugging!" says Poseidon.

"I'm tugging!" says Aphrodite.

"Pretty butterfly!" says Heracles.

"Heracles!" screams Adonis. "Stop butterflying and start tugging!"

Uh-oh.

Heracles gives one gentle pull—like he's opening a door or something—and the next thing you know, *mud happens.*

Oh, and for the record, mud tastes . . . muddy. I don't recommend it.

CHAPTER 2

"Congratulations, Team Gods. Victory is yours once more!" booms Principal Deadipus. "And to Team Odds—well, umm, thanks for playing our game."

6

Deadipus hands my brother a huge trophy, and then hands me . . . this.

"Thanks, Principal D," replies Adonis. "It was a tough fight, and the Oddballs were a worthy opponent. Wait—what am I saying? It wasn't tough at all! We wiped the floor with them! We'll wipe the floor with ANYONE!"

Just then a voice emerges from the stands. "Really? Care to back that up?"

"Who said that?" yells my brother.

A guy in a black toga, white shirt, black tie, and a black chauffeur's cap steps forward.

"Hear me now. I am Uberous, driver for Mercury, messenger of the *real* Gods—the *ROMAN* Gods. I carry with me a message from the *real* side of Mount Olympus—the *ROMAN* side. The *real* Mount Olympus Middle School—the *ROMAN* one— challenges you . . . to a tug-of-war."

Say whaaaaaaaat???

"You're all wet, pal!" yells Poseidon. "There's only one side to Mount O, and that's the Greek side!"

"Perhaps your principal should clue you in . . . *squirt*," replies Uberous. "There's a lot you don't seem to know."

"Is it true, Principal Deadipus?" asks my brainiac friend, Mathena. "Is there a Roman side to Mount Olympus?"

"Well . . . errr . . . you see," stammers Principal Deadipus. "Uhhh . . . *technically speaking*, Uberous is correct. There is another side of Mount Olympus."

"Why didn't you ever tell us about that?" asks Mathena. "Why didn't our *parents* tell us?"

"Because there's nothing to tell!" replies Deadipus. "Oh—but if you insist, here is a very condensed history lesson."

Every single boy—God and Odd alike—begins to giggle.

"What are you snickering about?" asks Deadipus.

"Hehe," replies Adonis. "You said . . . heeheehee . . . *Uranus* . . . heeheeheehee."

"Oh. My. Gods," says Deadipus. "Moving on."

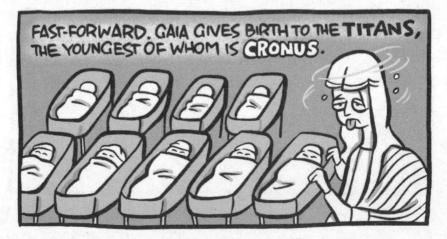

"But what about the Romans?" asks Mathena.

"The Romans are nobodies . . . pretenders . . . wannabes!" howls Deadipus. "We came first, and the Romans have been furious about it ever since!"

"We're not furious!" whines Uberous. "We're just second! We try harder!"

"The Romans have been challenging us *forever*," continues Deadipus. "And we've been rejecting them forever. I mean, really—why bother competing against a weak, sad, pathetic opponent? It only lessens you in the process!"

"Tell me about it!" says Adonis.

"And FYI, children, I know who sent Uberous here today," says Deadipus. "There's only one Roman who could be so resentful, and so jealous of me— and of *us*. It's been that way for eight hundred years."

"I don't get it," I say. "Who could be so awful to you?"

Deadipus sighs deeply. "My baby brother . . . Fredipus."

"Oh, your *brother*," I reply. "Now I get it."

CHAPTER 3

"**M**y brother always envied my success," Deadipus continues. "He constantly compared himself
to me. He talked like me, he dressed like me—
he wanted to *be* me. And when he saw that he
couldn't make it on the Greek side, he switched and
became . . . *Roman*. My father, Eggheadipus, was so
ashamed."

"It's so sad when a child's an embarrassment to
his father," says Adonis. "Isn't that right, Oddy?"

"For the last time," Deadipus says to Uberous, "please inform my poor, pitiful brother that the Greeks are not interested in playing *tug-of-war* with the Romans."

"Wait just a minute," interrupts Adonis. "Who says we're not interested?"

"History says!" replies Deadipus. "And so do I!"

"Well, *I* say it's time we had some new opponents around here," says Adonis. "We're at the top of our tug-of-war game! And I'm getting pretty tired of only having the Odd Gods around to clobber."

PFFFFFFFFFFFFFFFFFFFFFFFFFFFFTTTTTTTTT!!!! spews my gassy friend Gaseous.

Adonis stares at Gaseous. "You could've just said, 'Me too,' Fart Face!"

POOPS...
I MEAN
OOPS.

"Adonis is right!" says Aphrodite. "We need real competition!"

"Yeah, bring on the Romans!" agrees Poseidon. "We'll slaughter 'em!"

"Me like slaughter!" seconds Heracles.

I have to say, I'm pretty intrigued by this notion. I mean, not the *slaughter* part—but to think there's a whole group of kids out on Mount Olympus that we never even knew existed! Maybe they're nice. Who knows—maybe there are even Odds . . . like me!

"I think it would be fun," I say to Principal Deadipus. "What have we got to lose?"

"Oh, I don't know," replies Deadipus. "Our reputation? Our self-respect? Our dignity?"

"Dignity schmignity!" sneers my teeny pal Puneous. "Let's see what they've got!"

"You heard your students, Principal Deadipus," says Uberous. "Give 'em what they want! That is . . . unless you're *scared*."

Then Uberous starts taunting Deadipus by clucking like a chicken! That ruffles everyone's feathers—especially Mathena, our Odd Goddess of math and poultry, and her fowl friends, Clucky and Ducky!

"How dare you bawk at me, sir!" cries Deadi-pus. "Greek Gods . . . *scared*? Was Perseus scared of Medusa? Was Theseus scared of the Minotaur?"

"Were we scared of the Whyclops, Mumce, and the Sirens when we went on the Oddyssey?"* asks Adonis.

"TOTALLY!!!" reply the Odd Gods.

"Well, we're not scared now, Uberous," says Deadipus. "You tell Fredipus we are ready for the Romans anytime, anywhere. We'll give him a beatup he'll never forget!"

---

* *Odd Gods 2: The Oddyssey.* Available wherever books are sold!

"I think you mean beat*down*, sir," I say.

"*Whatever!*"

"Done," says Uberous. "The Romans will see you here in one week."

"Oh, snap!" replies Deadipus.

"Good one, Grandpa," mocks Uberous. He bows, tips his black cap, and sneers, "Later, Greeklings!"

"I hope I won't regret this," mutters Deadipus.

"Don't you worry, Deadly," says my brother. "Just leave it all up to me!"

Hmmm.

If I were Principal Deadipus, I'd already be regretting this!

CHAPTER 4

That night, Adonis spills the beans to our dad, Zeus, and our mom, Freya, about how the Romans challenged us to a tug-of-war. Meanwhile, I spill Mom's Norwegian specialty pølse'n'beans stew into my dog Trianus's mouth!

"The Romans?" Zeus chortles. "You're actually going to compete against the *Romans*? Those JV copycat losers have played second fiddle to us for years!"

"You know," says Mom, "it wouldn't be the worst thing to get along with them. Maybe we could have a big playdate!"

"A *playdate*!" snaps Dad. "Oh, please. And have to endure that so-called King of the Roman Gods, *Jupiter*? As if! He's so high and mighty! He thinks he's right about everything, and no one else matters. Can you imagine having to put up with someone like that?"

"Ja, that would be terrible," mutters Mom.

"I don't even know why we're allowing them to come here!" says Dad. "Blecchhh—Romans! They're so weird and . . . different!"

"They're not so different," scolds Mom. "Besides, even if they were—which they're not—what's so bad about being different? I'm a Norse Goddess. I'm different, aren't I?"

"Well . . . uhh . . . errr," sputters Dad. "That's different."

"I think different's kinda cool," I say.

"Of course you do!" replies my brother. "Because *you're* different!"

"And I wouldn't want my Oddy-Woddy any other way!" coos Mom.

Awwww! Thanks, Mom!

"Ewwww!" says Adonis. "Gross, Mom!"

"I don't like different," growls Dad. "I like *same*! *SAME* HAIR ON MY HEAD! *SAME* BEARD ON MY FACE! *SAME* SHEETS ON MY BED! *SAME* FOOD ON MY PLATE!"

"Dad's a poet, but he don't know it!" shouts Adonis.

"I've even worn the same toga for twenty years!" Dad proudly exclaims.

Speaking of gross . . .

TMI, DAD!!!

"And here's what else is going to stay the same: we're number one, and the Romans are number two." Then he turns to Adonis. "You better show them who's boss, son!"

"I read you loud and clear, O Great One!"

"That's my boy! And what are *you* going to do to the Romans, Oddonis?"

"Gee . . . I'm not sure," I reply. "Maybe bake them some cookies?"

CHAPTER 5

Why did I ever say I'd bake cookies? Now I'm in charge of snacks!

Okay, I know us Odd Gods aren't exactly world-class athletes, and we're not tug-of-war material, but still . . . .

"This stinks," mutters Puneous.

"Sorry," says Gaseous. "Big breakfast this morning."

"I don't mean you," replies Puneous. "I mean having to be pack mules for the Gods."

"You said id," agrees our sickly friend Germes, wiping his nose on a nectar bottle. "I'b got ambrosia holes, orange slices, *and* boddles of nectar. But here's de weird pard: not eben *one* of de Gods has asked me for a snack. Whad's up with dat?" Then he sneezes all over his ambrosia holes.

"It's a mystery, Germes," I say.

"Oh, nectar girl!" Aphrodite calls out to Mathena. "I do believe I'm feeling a bit parched over here. Won't you be a darling and come nectar me!"

"Grrrrrr," Mathena grumbles. "I'll nectar you, all right." She tells her poultry pals, Clucky and Ducky, to hang tight. Then she turns to Germes and says with a devilish grin, "Hey, Germes, mind if I switch nectar bottles with you?"

"Are you sure, Bathena?" Germes replies. "I just wiped my nose on id."

SNOT A PROBLEM... HEH, HEH...

"Hey, Odd Squad!" yells my brother. "Quit smirking and start working! I need more snacks—NOW!"

I lug the snacks over and find Adonis lying in the grass, daydreaming.

"*You* need a snack?" I say.

"Nah—Heracles does," says Adonis. "I just wanted to watch you carry them."

"Of course." I sigh. "But what about you? Isn't there some tugging or warring you should be doing too?"

"Ha!" cackles Adonis. "As long as Heracles is good, we've got this in the bag."

Hmmm. At least I don't have to carry them now!

Just then, we hear a rattling noise off in the distance and see a yellow school chariot approaching. OMG! It's the Romans! Principal Deadipus and Coach Gluteus Maximus gather us all together.

"All right, students," says Deadipus nervously, "the time has come. Just remember the immortal words of Heraclitus: 'Character is destiny.'"

"Huh?" says Adonis.

"Umm . . . how about the immortal words of Homer: 'Ever to excel'?"

"What?" says Poseidon.

"Uhhh . . . the immortal words of Aesop: 'The unlucky man will be bitten even by a sheep'?"

"Coach, can you throw me a bone here?" whispers Deadipus.

"Yo, Gods!" screams Coach Gluteus Maximus. "Let's kick some Roman rump!"

"OH, YEAAAAAAHHHHHHHHHHHH!!!" roar the Gods.

In the immortal words of *me*: "What fools these Greek Gods be!"

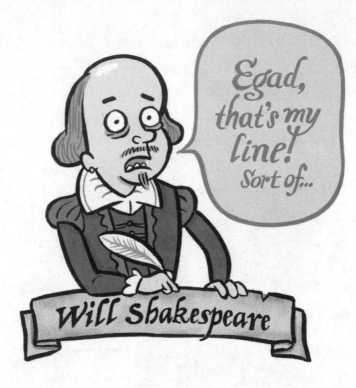

CHAPTER 6

The door of the Romans' school chariot swings open, and out pops a spry old dude with a microphone in his hand.

"Hi-o, you kooky kids! I'm Sol, the Roman school chariot driver. Some folks tell me I've got a Roman nose. Why? Because it's roamin' all over my face! Thank you! I'm also Roman God of the sun—hey, speaking of the sun, it's so hot out . . ."

"How hot is it?" yell voices from inside the chariot.

"It's so hot, chickens are laying hard-boiled eggs! Thank you!"

"But enough about me." Sol grabs Deadipus's hand and pulls him forward. "How ya doin'? What's your name, sir?"

"I am Principal Deadipus."

"So *you're* Deadipus?" says Sol. "Your brother Fredipus told me all about you! Hey, are you still afraid of the dark?"

"Well, I never!" gasps Deadipus.

"I'm kidding! I kid!" chuckles Sol. "Whoa, Deadipus! Maybe you should put a little protein in your diet. You're nothing but skin and bones . . . without the skin! Thank you! And speaking of bones: Why couldn't the skeleton fart in front of his friends?"

"I don't know," replies Deadipus. "Why?"

"Because he didn't have the guts!"

"Good one, Sol!" snorts Gaseous. "HA HA HA!" *BWWWONNNNNNNNKKKKKK!!!*

"I see nothing funny about that!" says Deadipus. "Where is Fredipus?"

"You want him? You got him!"

Deadipus turns to all of us and whispers, "Get ready, everyone! Wait until you see my sad little brother! I'll bet he's still trying to be like me!"

"Put your hands together," Sol thunders, "and say hello to Frrrrrrrrredipus!"

"F-F-F-F-Freddy?" stammers Deadipus.

"Hello, Deady, you old fuddy-duddy," says Fredipus.

"You look good, Freddy. I mean . . . really good. Wh-wh-what happened?"

"Simple," replies Fredipus. "Romans rule!"

"I beg your pardon," snaps Deadipus. "But *Greeks* rule!"

"We'll see about that," sneers Fredipus. "Sol, introduce our team."

"Sure thing, boss!" says Sol. "Ladies and germs . . ."

"Did he say germs?" asks Germes excitedly.

"Please give a warm welcome to our pillars of pulling, our heroes of hauling, our deities of dragging: YOUR Roman Mount Olympus Middle School Tug-of-War Team!!!"

THE GOD OF LIGHT,
APOLLO!

THE GOD OF THE SEAS,
NEPTUNE!

THE GODDESS OF BEAUTY,
VENUS!

THE GOD OF STRENGTH,
HERCULES!

AND OUR COACH,
TRAPEZIUS!

None of us can believe what we're seeing. The Roman Gods aren't just legit . . . they're almost exact copies of the Greek Gods! My brother and his crew are speechless. They just stare, dumbfounded, at their Roman doppelgängers.*

"Wow," mutters Mathena. "It's two times the Gods!"

"Yeah," agrees Puneous. "Double the dopes!"

"Umm . . . you guys?" I say. "It's not just the Gods who've multiplied. Look!"

"Well, I'll be a fanny frog!" gasps Gaseous. "They look like . . . like . . ."

"Us!" we all say.

---

* *Doppelgängers! Great word!*

CHAPTER 7

While the Gods and the coaches give each other some serious stinkeye, and Deadipus and Fredipus reignite their fraternal feud, the Odds and I decide to say hello to our fellow nectar bearers. Gaseous is the first one of us to break the ice . . . by breaking wind.

PFFFFFFFFFFFFFFFFFFFFFFFFTTTTTTTTTTT!
"What's shakin', homeys? I'm Gaseous."

"*BURRRRRRRRRRRRRRRPPPPPPPPPPPPPPP!*" replies a kid. "Hi, Gaseous. I'm Belchous."

"Whoa!" says Gaseous. "Nice tone, dude!"

"Oh my, oh my, oh my," says a girl standing next to Belchous. "I hope those smells don't get on my skin or my hair or my toga! Then everyone will blame me for being gassy or burpy and they won't let me back on the chariot and I'll have to walk all the way back home and there'll be snakes everywhere and I'll get eaten by the snakes and I'll miss dinner and my parents will kill me! Hello, I'm Minervous."

"Boy, that escalated quickly," says Mathena.

"Hey—I'm Mathena. Don't be nervous. Gaseous's farts aren't silent, and they aren't deadly."

"I don't smell a thing!" says a girl's voice from . . . the sky.

I look up, and up, and up, and up some more.

"Hi down there!" she calls. "I'm Heightania!"

"Oh, great," mutters Puneous. "A tall girl. Of course she doesn't smell anything—her nose is in the stratosphere!"

"Mmmmb," says another girl, taking a big whiff. "I think id smells sweed. Heddo eberybody—by name is Bacteria."

"Say whaaaaaaad?" wheezes Germes. "Greedings, Bacteria! I'b Germes!"

Hmmm. Talk about a gruesome twosome!

"Hmmm," says the last kid in the group. "Talk about an infection connection."

"Good one," I laugh. The kid lifts his head, and I'm staring straight at . . .

"Uhhh . . . hi," I say. "I'm Oddonis."

"Uhhh . . . hi," the kid says. "I'm Oddpollo."

"My dad is Zeus, and my brother's Adonis. But I'm not like them."

"My dad is Jupiter, and my brother's Apollo. But I'm not like them, either."

"I'm what's known around here as an Odd God,"
I say. "We all are."

"Really?" Oddpollo replies. "Where we're from,
they call us odd, but they sure don't think of us as
Gods."

"Roman Odd Gods!" whoops Gaseous. "I'll"—
BRRRRRRAAAACK—"to that!"

"And I'll BRRRRRPPPPPPPP to it!" adds Belchous.

Meanwhile, I can't stop staring at my reflection—
I mean, Oddpollo. Same goes for him.

"Hmmm," we both murmur at the same time.
"Jinx!"

"SORRY TO INTERRUPT THE DORKFEST!" screams Adonis. "I can't tell which one of you losers is my brother, but I'm gettin' thirsty over here! One of you dweebs better bring me some nectar . . . *PRONTO!*"

"YEAH!" echoes Oddpollo's brother, Apollo. "WHAT HE SAID!"

Oddpollo and I both sigh, roll our eyes, and say, "Oh, *brothers.*"

CHAPTER 8

By the time we drag all the snacks over to the Gods, they've already lined up for the tug-of-war. The stinkeye staredown between the two sides hasn't stopped, and now—thanks to Adonis and Apollo—they're trash-talking, too.

"How's it feel to be second . . . *NUMBER TWO?*" sneers Adonis.

"That's enough, Adonis," scolds Deadipus while glaring at Fredipus. "There's no need for name-calling—especially when our team is *so superior to theirs.*"

"Hey, I'd rather be a Roman God than a *Geek* God!" responds Apollo.

"Hold your tongue, Apollo," chastises Fredipus, glaring back at Deadipus. "Better to vanquish *an inferior foe* with deeds rather than words."

"Ready, teams?" bark Coach Gluteus Maximus and Coach Trapezius. Their whistles are in their mouths, and they're elbowing each other for position. Geez—get a grip, grown-ups!

"On the count of three!" yells Deadipus.

"THREE TWO ONE GO!!!" screams Fredipus.

And the tug-a-thon begins.

"Give it all you got, Gods!" cries Adonis.

"Pull, Romans, pull!" shouts Apollo. "Let's beat these clod Gods!"

Both teams yank, drag, and jerk with all their might, but they're so evenly matched, the rope doesn't move a daktylos (that's a Greek inch)! It's clear that the Gods are equal *physically*, so my brother decides to challenge the Romans *mentally* (*really* not his strong suit, IMHO).

"Hey, Apollo," taunts Adonis midtug, "instead of the God of light, they should call you the God of lightweights!"

"Well, if you ask me," mocks Apollo, "I don't see how you can be called the God of beauty when you've got a big zit on your nose!"

"WHAAAAAAT???" shrieks Adonis. "A ZIT!!! WHERE? WHERE???"

Adonis drops the rope and begins running around like a chicken with its head cut off . . . and a pimple on its beak.

"WHO'S GOT A MIRROR?" screeches Adonis. "I NEED A MIRROR!"

"Adonis! Get back here!" calls Poseidon.

"EMERGENCY! SOMEONE CALL IX-I-I!!!" howls Adonis. "GET ME A DERMATOLOGIST . . . STAT!"

"Can't . . . hold . . . on . . . ," groans Heracles.

Even mighty Heracles can't save our side this time. The Romans, anchored by Hercules, give the rope one last tug, and the Greeks—except, that is, for my still-hysterical brother—go tumbling into the muck. All of the Gods are shocked and awed! And so are the Odds!

"Here's mud in your eye," Oddpollo whispers to me. "And nose, and mouth, and hair, and ears . . ."

"Been there, done that," I whisper back, "and once was enough!"

CHAPTER 9

"**H**OORAY!!!!" thunders Fredipus. "EAT DIRT, DEADY!"

Fredipus, Coach Trapezius, and the Roman Gods are dancing and hugging, celebrating their stunning victory. Meanwhile, our side is experiencing the bitter taste of defeat . . . and mud. And they know exactly who's responsible.

Principal Deadipus, seething mad, turns to Fredipus and fumes, "I cry foul! Your player goaded our player!"

"I cry boo-hoo!" replies Fredipus. "In case you didn't notice, your player goaded first! Adonis was the goader! Is it our fault he's a lousy goadee?"

"But but but," Deadipus whines, "it's not FAIR!"

"You know what isn't fair?" answers Fredipus. "You Greeks thinking you're better than us all these years!" Fredipus gathers his team and turns back to his still-boiling brother. "It's been *super* seeing you again, Deady," he teases. "Now, if you'll excuse us, we have to get back to the *winning* side of Mount Olympus. Jupiter is going to be so happy when he hears the news!"

I know someone who is going to be so *UNhappy* when he hears the news!

The Romans file onto their chariot, still whooping it up.

"Hate to *beat and run*," Sol wisecracks, "but we gotta make like a bakery truck and haul buns! Thank you!"

I feel a tap on my shoulder and turn to see Oddpollo and the other Roman Rejects waiting to say goodbye.

"Nice meeting you, Oddonis," says Oddpollo. "I hope I see you again."

"Me too, Oddpollo," I reply. "But after what just happened, I'm not holding my breath."

"Speaking of breath," declares Belchous, "*BURRRRRRRRRRPPPPPPPPPP!* That one's for you, Gaseous!"

BWWWWWAAAAACCCKKKK! "Back at ya, Belchous!" gasses Gaseous.

"We can't miss the chariot! We can't miss the chariot! We CANNOT miss the chariot!" wails Minervous.

"Close your eyes and count chickens," whispers Mathena. "That always calms me down."

"Don't you mean sheep?" says Minervous.

"Trust me," replies Mathena, winking at Clucky.

"Can you say goodbye to Puneous for me, you

guys?" yells Heightania. "I can't find him anywhere!"

"I'm right here, Gigantaur!" grumbles Puneous. "Get
some binoculars!"

"I made you dis, Bacteria," sniffles Germes. "Id's
a friendship ring . . . worm."

"Id's disgusting, Gerbes," snuffles Bacteria, putting the ringworm on her finger. "And I love id!"

As our new friends board their chariot for home,
it occurs to me that life sure is funny sometimes.
For a day that started out so bad, it ended up being

pretty good! In a total switcheroo, the only ones who had a bad day were my brother and his crew. And if I know my dad, the day's about to get a whole lot worse . . . for all of them!

CHAPTER 10

"**W**E . . . WE . . . LOST??? TO . . . TO . . . THE ROMANS???"

You can literally hear Principal Deadipus's bones rattling as he tries to explain.

"We were t-t-tied, Your Greatness," Deadipus stammers, "until . . . shall we say . . . *extenuating circumstances* arose."

"The Romans played dirty, Pops!" cries Adonis. "Apollo provoked me!"

"That's zit, Adonis!" I add. "You hit it right on the nose!"

Adonis whips his head around at me and hisses, "Not funny, Oddball!"

"Oh, *I see*, Adonis," Dad says, pacing the floor. "Apollo provoked *you*. And you didn't say anything to him first?"

"Ummm . . ." Adonis hems and haws. "Not that I can recall?"

"That's good. Because it would be so unfortunate if you said something that caused him to respond, which then caused you to drop the rope and run around yelling for a doctor because you thought you had A PIMPLE!"

"How did you know?" Adonis gasps.

"HELLO!!!" bellows Dad. "I'm ZEUS!!!"

"I'm sorry, O Grand Forgiver," Adonis says. "But trust me: I've learned my lesson."

"And what lesson is that?"

"That I am the God of beauty and desire, and there's no way I could ever get a zit!"

"What do we do now, Deadipus?" asks Dad. "Olympus is going to want answers!"

"Well, Your Magnificence," replies Deadipus,

"I've given it a great deal of thought, and I see two ways to handle this situation."

"Yes?"

"Either we say aliens took over the Gods' bodies during the tug-of-war, but everything is fine now, or . . ."

"Yes, yes?"

"We say Zeus is out of town and you are his twin brother named Meus who had nothing to do with it. Wearing these 'Meus' antlers should help."

"Not bad," murmurs Meus . . . I mean, Zeus.

"Why don't you just ask for a do-over?" I say.

"What did you say?!?" Dad asks.

"Tell the Romans you want another chance. What do you have to lose?"

"Why, that's *brilliant*, Oddonis!" Dad splutters. "Whose idea was that?"

"Nobody's," I reply. "I thought of it myself."

"Riiiiiight," says Dad. "That's your story, and you're sticking to it."

"It's not a story—it's the truth!"

"If you say so, Oddonis. But I want more than a do-over. I come here to bury the Romans, not to praise them."

Will Shakespeare

"I say we challenge the Romans to an athletic competition the likes of which the world has never seen!" Dad declares. "An all-day festival of sport, with the winner to be crowned best middle school on all Olympus!"

"Brilliant, sire!" gushes Deadipus.

"But we'll need a catchy name," muses Dad. "Something that blends the unifying spirit of sportsmanship with the inspiring power of athletics. Something like . . . the Zeuper Bowl!"

"How about AdonisMania?" crows Adonis.

"Or PimplePalooza!" I chirp.

"Wide World of Zeus!" Dad roars. "ZeusSportsCenter!"

"I've got it!" squeals Deadipus. "Zeussical!"

"Why don't you just call it the Olympics?" I say. "Or the Olympic Games? You know, because it's happening on Mount *Olympus*?"

"The *Olympics*," chortles Dad. "That's the silliest name I've ever heard!"

"But—"

"Wait! I know!" Dad exclaims. "We'll call it the *Godlympics*!"

"Genius!" cries Deadipus. "You've done it again, Your Highness!"

Oh, come on! You've gotta be kidding me!

CHAPTER 11

Dad proposes a face-to-face, God-to-God meeting between him and Jupiter.

Intense negotiations begin. When and where will the meeting take place? Which Gods will attend? What snacks will be served? (And will I have to carry the snacks again?)

Of course Dad won't set foot on the Roman side of Mount Olympus, and Jupiter won't come to the Greek side, so that complicates things even further. By the time it's all worked out, the messenger Gods—Hermes and Mercury—are all worn out!

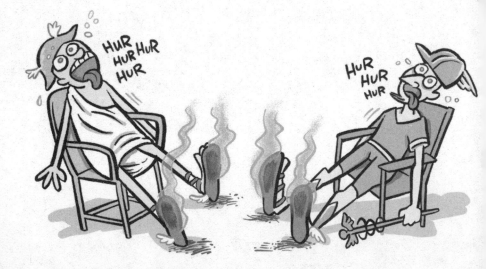

Meanwhile, Mom thinks this is all one big mistake.

"Der er ugler i mosen!" she says to Dad.

(Okay, what she's saying in Norwegian is "There are owls in the moss!" but what she means is, "Something is off!")

"What's the problem?" replies Dad.

"The problem is, you can't stand Jupiter—why, I do not know," says Mom. "And it is *impossible* for you to keep your cool! I see this ending very badly."

"Stop worrying, Freya," says Dad. "Deadipus will be with me, and if it makes you feel any better, I'll bring Adonis too."

"YES!!!" screams Adonis. "I'll DESTROY them with my negotiating!"

"That doesn't make me feel better." Mom sighs. "Bring Oddonis. He's the only one of you with a hjerne in his hode!"

(That's Norwegian for "a brain in his head." Takk, Mom!)

"OKAY!" barks Dad.

"NOKAY!" groans Adonis.

So, the next day, at the EXACT borderline between the Greek and Roman sides of Mount Olympus, the meeting finally takes place. We sit on our side of the border, and the Romans sit on theirs.

If you ask me, grown-ups can be so juvenile! But at least I get to see Oddpollo again!

"This must be quite embarrassing for you, Zeus," mutters Jupiter.

"Embarrassing?" snaps Zeus. "Why would you say that?"

"You know—after suffering that humiliating defeat in the tug-of-war?"

"Quite right," agrees Fredipus. "Mortifying, really."

"I'll mortify you, really!" hisses Deadipus.

"On the plus side," adds Apollo, "you can barely see Adonis's zit now!"

"I DON'T HAVE A ZIT!" moans Adonis.

"Can we focus, please?" I beg.

"Yes, please?" seconds Oddpollo.

"Grrrrrrrrrrrright," Dad grumbles. "Principal Deadipus, you may present our proposal on my behalf."

"With pleasure, O *Greatest* One," replies Deadipus. He clears his throat and announces, "We the anointed, original inhabitants of Mount Olympus, challenge you, our newbie neighbors, to the first-ever Godlympic Games: a one-day celebration of athletic achievement, with the winner to be named best on all Olympus. What say you to this challenge?"

The Romans huddle up, and after a brief conference, Fredipus responds, "We accept your Godlympic Games challenge."

"Well, that wasn't so hard, was it?" Dad says proudly.

"There's just one small thing," says Jupiter.

"And what is that?" Dad asks.

"Well, we *did* win the tug-of-war—" says Jupiter.

"Through trickery!" accuses Deadipus.

"And zittery!" I add.

"ACK!!!" wails Adonis.

"And since we won," Jupiter continues, "we really don't need these *Godlympics* to decide who is best on Olympus. I think we all know."

"What are you getting at, Jupiter?" asks Dad.

"I'm just saying . . . let's raise the stakes a bit, shall we?"

"Papa, please," Oddpollo hisses at Jupiter. "You know what Mamma said."

"Enough, Oddpollo!" snaps Jupiter. "Daddy's got this."

"How about this, Zeus old boy?" asks Jupiter. "If we win, Greek yogurt will forever be called Roman yogurt!"

"FINE!" counters Zeus. "And if we win, Roman numerals will forever be called Greek numerals!"

"FINE!" roars Jupiter. "But why stop there? Let's make things really interesting: the winner gets half of the loser's kingdom!"

"You want to make things INTERESTING?" Zeus thunders. "You want to RAISE THE STAKES? Well, how about these stakes, *old boy*? The winner gets ALL OF OLYMPUS, and the loser has to LEAVE!"

"DEAL!" Jupiter bellows.

"Wh-wh-what just happened?" I whisper to Odd-pollo.

"I was going to ask you the same thing!" Oddpollo whispers back.

"What did we do?" I say.

"*We* didn't do anything," says Oddpollo. "*They* did!"

"And they're going to hear about it," I reply.

We heave a big sigh and say together, "Oh, *mothers*."

CHAPTER 12

Remember that volcanic explosion Dad had after we lost the tug-of-war? Here's Mom's version when she finds out what Dad did.

"Å VÆRE FØDT BAK EN BRUNOST!" Mom roars.

(That's Norwegian for "To be born behind brown cheese." Actual meaning? To be *stupid*.)

"Don't tell me I was born behind brown cheese!" Dad yells. "For your information, I was raised by nymphs on the island of Naxos and fed with milk and honey from the broken-off horn of a goat nurse! So there!"

"You bet our HOME!" cries Mom. "Jupiter baited you, and you bet EVERYTHING on some foolish middle school games!"

"Godlympic Games!" answers Dad. "Which we are going to win!"

"You mean like the tug-of-war you said we'd win?" asks Mom.

"We had a pimple problem there," Dad replies, giving Adonis an eyeful. "Plus, we took our opponents for granted, and we didn't prepare. This time we are going to train like no one has ever trained before. We'll train XXIV/VII, day and night, rain or shine. We'll train until the cows come home. And other cliches! When we're through, the Twelve Labors of Heracles will feel like afternoon chores to these weak and lazy kids!"

"So because you lost your temper, the children have to suffer?" Mom says.

"Wisdom comes through suffering!" Dad argues. "And they'll emerge wisdomer than any Roman!"

"I kinda like the Romans," I say. "Oddpollo's cool."

That might not have been the wisdomest thing I've ever said.

"*Oh, really,* Oddonis," Dad sneers. "Let's start your training now."

"Oddy's the one who likes the Romans," groans Adonis. "Why do I have to pull this stupid oxcart too?"

"*Zit's* pretty obvious, don't you think, son?" replies Dad.

Adonis and I cart Dad around all afternoon. After hours of trudging back and forth, Adonis and I are so loopy that we start to feel like actual oxen. So, we do what any boys in our situation would do: we make cow jokes.

70

"How does a cow become invisible?" I ask.

"With ca*moo*flage!" Adonis answers. "What do you call a cow that plays an instrument?"

"A *moo*-sician!" I snicker. "Where do baby cows go for lunch?"

"The *calf*eteria!" Adonis giggles. "What do you call a cow with a nervous twitch?"

"Beef jerky!" I chortle. "Where do cows put their paintings?"

"In the *moo*-seum!" he snorts.

"STOP! STOP! STOP!" moans Dad. "I can't take it anymore!"

"You're right, Dad," we reply. "This is . . . udder nonsense!"

Hard to believe, but Adonis and I actually have fun together, for the first time, like, EVER. Maybe this training program won't be so bad after all. Moo knows?

CHAPTER 13

Okay, I've got a serious beef with this training program.

We have breakfast in the dark. Totally weird—but the one good thing is that I don't have to look at Mom's oatmeal while I eat it!

"Why do we have to be up now, Dad?" Adonis complains. "The school chariot won't be here for an hour!"

"Chariot?" Dad scoffs. "You're not riding to school, boys—you're *running*. As soon as you're done with your oatmeal."

"Why must my precious Oddy do this?" asks Mom. "He's no athlete!"

I know she didn't mean it the way it came out, but Mom's right!

"Every child on Mount Olympus must train," Dad says. "No exceptions, no mercyyyyyy!"

After breakfast, Dad stands outside and watches as Adonis and I run to school. Check that: we run until we're sure Dad can't see us anymore, and then we walk. Grumpily.

"This sucks!" Adonis grouses. "I get how *you* need to train, but *I* shouldn't have to. I'm an Adonis!"

"That's the kind of thinking that got us into this mess!" I snap. "If you hadn't been so worried about how you look, maybe you wouldn't have lost the tug-of-war and Dad wouldn't have made that bet and we'd still be asleep right now!"

"You'll never know how hard it is to be as beautiful as me, Oddy." He sighs.

I'm about to take out the world's smallest violin when I notice a commotion happening outside school. Everybody—and I mean everybody—is there. Students, teachers, workers, you name it. Adonis spots his God peeps and does his usual "I-don't-know-who-you-are" ditching of me. I find my Odd pals standing near Principal Deadipus, Coach Gluteus Maximus, and Ms. Meticulous. The grown-ups look like they're about to give a speech. Oh, and they also look *ridiculous*.

"Settle, please," drones Deadipus. "Attention, everyone. By order of our supreme leader, Zeus, school will hereby be canceled until further notice."

Commence whooping and hollering and . . .

BWWWWWOOOOOOOONNNNKKKKKK!!!

. . . some festive farting, too.

"This is the greatest day ever!" hoots (and toots) Gaseous.

"No *school*?" Mathena asks anxiously. "Does that mean no . . . no . . . *math*?"

"That's the sum of it, dearie!" replies Ms. Meticulous.

"NOOOOOOOOOOOOO!!!!!!!!" cries Mathena.

"YESSSSSSSSSSSSSSSSSS!!!!!!!!" cries Gaseous. Tears are streaming down both of their faces—but for totally different reasons.

"Silence!" barks Deadipus. "Let me finish. School will be canceled and *replaced* . . . by an intensive program of physical exercise, in preparation for the first-ever Godlympic Games. We will be competing against the Romans—and the stakes could not be higher."

Ya think, Principal D? You've heard of Go Big or Go Home? That's nothing compared to Go Big or Lose Your Home!

CHAPTER 14

The other Odd Gods and I are super-stressed about this "intensive program of physical exercise." See, sports have never really been our thing.

I've already had a taste of my dad's training program, and I am NOT a fan. Will this be better . . . or worse? Principal Deadipus clears things up by introducing us to this gray-haired guy with surprisingly muscular arms and legs.

"Attention, students," he says. "Please give a warm MOM welcome to our first guest instructor: Sisyphus!"

"Thanks, Principal Deadipus, and hello, future Godlympians!" states Sisyphus. "I am Sisyphus, and I'm here to coach you on your first drill of the day. You could say it's a workout I know all too well, because I've been cursed to do it for all eternity. It's pretty simple: together, you all are going to push a rock up a hill."

That's it? We all breathe a sigh of relief . . . until we see Sisyphus's rock.

"Mathematically impossible!" declares Mathena.

"Trust me," replies Sisyphus. "It can be done."

"Piece of cake!" says Adonis. "Heracles, do your stuff!"

"Sorry, troops—no Heracles," declares Coach Gluteus Maximus. "He won't be allowed to compete in every event, so you'll all have to pick up the slack."

"NO HERACLES?" we all scream.

"Why you say 'NO, HERACLES'?" replies Heracles. "What Heracles do?"

"Largest in front, smallest in the back," Sisyphus says to us.

"Why the smallest in back?" complains Puneous.

"So you won't get stepped on, Ant-Boy!" mocks Adonis. "All right, everybody, take your places! Let's rock and roll!"

"And what are you going to do?" I ask my brother.

"Supervise, of course!" he replies.

"No dice, Adonis," says the coach. "Father's orders."

"Rats!" grumbles Adonis.

We line up behind Sisyphus's rock and start pushing. Unfortunately, the rock doesn't seem to notice. It just keeps sitting there.

"Use your legs!" yells Sisyphus. "Put your backs into it!"

You know what's worse than pushing a giant boulder up a hill? Pushing a giant boulder up a hill when you're standing right behind Gaseous!

"This . . . hot air," gags Aphrodite, "is taking the curl out of my hair!"

"I'd be habby to switch places wid you," says Germes.

"Less talking, more pushing!" shouts Coach.

Ever so slowly, we move the rock up the hill. We're making progress, until . . .

"Almost there!" calls Sisyphus. "Shove it!"

"YOU SHOVE IT!" Puneous yells back.

Puneous gives one last giant push from the back of the pack, and we heave the rock up on top of the hill. Success!!!

"We did it!" I croak.

"Way to go, team!" calls Sisyphus. "You *ROCK!*"

"Very funny," growls Puneous. "Thank Gods we'll never have to do THAT again!"

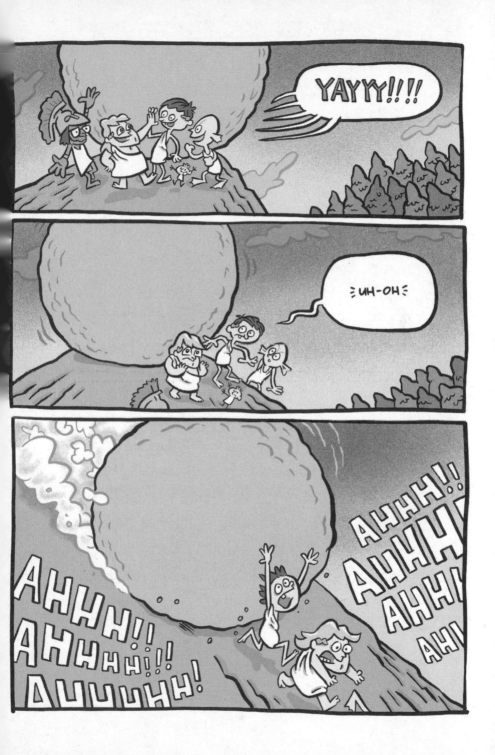

CHAPTER 15

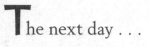The next day . . .

"Rock around the clock!" cries Sisyphus.

"Okay, that's it!" Puneous declares. "We are not doing this ANYMORE!"

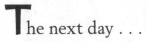
The next day . . .

"Rock out!" shouts Sisyphus.

"We rocked your world, rock!" Puneous roars. "I DARE
YOU to roll down again!!!"

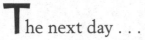he next day . . .

"Rock on!" screams Sisyphus.

After we push the rock up the hill one more time (and the rock chases us down the hill one more time), Principal Deadipus can see that we've all hit rock bottom. So he and his torture team pile on even more exercise!

"Students," announces Deadipus, "please say hello to our next guest instructor: the Greek Goddess of victory . . . Nike!"

"Awwww, are you a little tie-tie from pushing that teeny pebble up that tiny hill?" Nike asks us. "Well, TOO BAD—because we're just getting started! You are going to run and jump and throw and sweat like you've never run, jumped, thrown, or sweated in your entire entitled lives! You're going to hate it at first—heck, you might even hate me—but you're going to do it anyway. Did you hear me? All of you: Just Do It™!"

"What if we're gassy?" asks Gaseous.

"Just Do It™!" screams Nike.

"Whad if we're sickly?" asks Germes.

"Just Do It™!" screams Nike.

"What if we have no athletic skills whatsoever and are only here because of our bonehead brother and foolish father?" I ask.

"JUST DO IT™!!!" screams Nike.

Oh, well—then I guess we're just doing it™. Nike tells us to pick an instructor and break into groups to begin our training.

"Hey, you guys!" whispers Gaseous to the rest of the Odds. "I don't know about you, but that Nike scares me!"

"She freaks me oud!" gasps Germes.

"Well, Coach Gluteus Maximus isn't going to be any better!" I hiss.

"Let's get in Ms. Meticulous's group!" says Gaseous. "She's *ancient*! How hard can she be?"

"I agree with Gaseous," says Mathena. "Plus, if we're lucky, maybe she'll give us some math problems!"

"You never stop, do you?" mutters Puneous.

We follow Ms. Meticulous to the school track. We're figuring she'll take us on a nice leisurely walk. Then maybe we'll do some old-fogey stuff like bird-watching, gardening, a little shuffleboard, and after all that "strenuous" activity, a long nap, right?

WRONG!

Ms. Meticulous is a BEAST! By the end of the day, we can barely walk.

"'Let's get in Ms. Meticulous's group!'" Puneous jeers at Gaseous. "'She's ancient! How hard can she be?'"

"I did not see that comin'!" replies Gaseous.

"She totally schooled us," I say.

"She bead us into de ground," agrees Germes.

"Plus, she didn't give us any math!" moans Mathena.

Gaseous and I limp home together. On the way, we can't help noticing that Olympus is starting to look a little . . . different.

Nectarade

OFFICIAL SPORTS DRINK OF THE GODLYMPIC GAMES

"Nectarade?" I say.

"Official sports drink of the Godlympic Games?" echoes Gaseous. "What is happening here?"

"I don't know," I reply. "But I'll bet you my dad does."

CHAPTER 18

I hobble into my house and hear Dad's voice booming out from behind the closed door of his study.

"You tell Ambrosia O's that if they want a piece of these games, they're going to have to pony up! Otherwise, we'll get another official cereal for our Godlympics!"

I shuffle into the kitchen and ask my mom, "What's going on?"

"Your father is having a marketing meeting with Plutus, God of wealth and abundance," Mom says. "More like God of greed, if you ask me."

"They're marketing the Godlympics?" I say.

"Mm-hmm," replies Mom. "Did you see your father's Nectarade ad? I think he looks like an esel."

Speaking of esels, Adonis walks in and . . . wow . . . words escape me. . . .

"Check me out!" he brays. "Official sunglasses, official high-top sandals, and official Godlympic Games helmet!"

"You look officially idiotic," I say.

"Mom, could you please ignore the official loser of the Godlympic Games and make me a sandwich?"

"I won't ignore your brother, but I can make you a sandwich, Adonis," Mom says. "Smørbrød, as usual?"

"Smørbrød? No way!" Adonis replies indignantly. "Gimme olive loaf! It's the official lunch meat of the Godlympic Games!"

Officially SMH! "If you'll excuse me," I say, "I'm going to drag my aching body down to Fryonysus's and get some unoffical food in an unoffical diner."

SORE MUSCLES, BRO? TRY **ADONISIN!** IT'S THE OFFICIAL PAIN RELIEVER OF THE **GODLYMPIC GAMES!**

"ARRRGGGGGGGGGHHHHHHHH!"

Whenever I'm having a bad day (like today!), I can always count on Fryonysus to turn my mood around. He's like an island of calm in a sea of madness. As I enter his diner, I heave a happy sigh. I know I'll be able to tune out for a while, especially now that Fryonysus's is the official diner of the Godlympic Games. Wait—whaaaaat?

Say it ain't so, Fryo!

"Hey, Oddy!" cries Fryonysus, wrapping me up in his stockpile of arms. "Pop a squat next to your pals and I'll grab you some grub!"

The gang's all here—and the gang looks awful. Gaseous, Mathena, Puneous, and Germes are splayed out in our usual booth. Their plates of food sit in front of them, untouched.

"I'b hungry," murmurs Germes, "but I'b too tired to lift my fork!"

"It took me an hour to climb up to this booth!" moans Puneous.

"I fell asleep on my abacus," groans Mathena. "Now I've got lines all over my face!"

"I'm so pooped," Gaseous whimpers, "I can't even toot!"

"That's the only good news I've heard," I say. "This is crazy, you guys. If you ask me, this whole Godlympics thing is getting way out of control."

"Ya think?" Mathena replies. "My mom's putting *so* much pressure on me! Oh, and she wants her owl to be the official bird of the Godlympic Games!"

"I think my dad's eagle already claimed that." I sigh.

"My parents bug me every day!" Puneous says. "'How fast did you go today? Are you going to win? Will we have to move?' They make me so mad that I'm short with them all the time!"

"I never thought I'd hear myself say this," I add, "but I'd rather be back in school!"

"You know I would!" adds Mathena.

"I miss de lice id my locker," mutters Germes. "And I'b sick of dese goofy games!"

"I don't even want to *think* about them anymore!" Gaseous growls.

Just then, Fryonysus emerges from his kitchen carrying five plates.

"For my favorite athletes, your favorite treat!" he says. "Onion rings!"

"They're the official fried food of the Godlympic Games!"

Hmmm.

On second thought, make that *WAAAAAAAH-HHHHHHHHHHHHHH!!!!!*

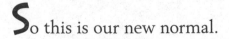

CHAPTER 19

So this is our new normal.

And so is this.

Adonis and I stumble into our house at the end of another grueling day. We're beyond beat. But that doesn't seem to faze Dad.

"Nike tells me she's very disappointed," Dad says. "She wants you all to—

"Let me guess," I reply. "Just Do It™?"

"Ms. Meticulous's reports about you aren't exactly glowing, Oddonis," says Dad. "But you're not as important as your brother—

"Unnskylld meg?" snaps Mom. (That's "Excuse me?" in Norwegian.)

"I mean athletically!" barks Dad. "Adonis and the other Gods are our top dogs! Our big cheeses! Our head honchos!"

"Well, this dog's going to lie down for a while," Adonis says with a yawn.

"Not today, son," replies Dad. "You and Trianus are doing an ad for MVPees—the official wee-wee pads of the Godlympic Games! After that, you have an interview with *Gods Illustrated* magazine, a private training session with the coach, then an ice bath, a quick dinner, and straight to bed. Remember: you've got a IV:00 run tomorrow morning!"

"Yes, sir," answers Adonis dejectedly.

Yikes. For once, I'm happy I stink at sports!

I feel bad for Adonis, though. Dad keeps pushing and pushing and pushing him. It's like these Godlympics—which were supposed to be *our* thing—have become *Dad's* thing now. It kinda takes the fun out of it, ya know? I hate to say it, but it even kind of makes me wish I were Roman. I'll bet they're not going crazy over this stuff!

Just then, the doorbell rings and I open the door to find . . . more stuff!

"Special delivery!" says Hermes.

"Are all these for us?" I ask.

"For your dad." Hermes sighs. "Official merchandise."

"This is nuts," I say.

"You're telling me!" complains Hermes. "Ever since the games were announced, everyone's been buying this junk around the clock! I haven't stopped for a minute! What do they think I am—some kind of *Amazon*???"

"I'm sorry, Hermes."

"Thanks."

"I'm also sorry you have to wear that scarf."

"Yeah," says Hermes. "Your dad told me he'd name it after me if I wore it. Hermes: the official scarf of the Godlympic Games. Oh, and I almost forgot: there's a letter for you, too. Cute stamp."

Oddpollo
XXI Jupiter Street
Roman Mount Olympus

FOREVER

Oddonis
I Zeus Boulevard
Greek Mount Olympus

Oddpollo sent me a letter! Me! I've NEVER gotten a letter! (I mean, except from my mom—which of course doesn't count.) But why is Oddpollo writing me?

CHAPTER 20

Dear Oddy,

Hey, it's Oddpollo. How's it going? I'm fine.

Oh, one more thing:

HELP!!!!!!!!!!!!!!!!!!!!!!!

Everyone here has gone completely cuckoo! My dad is OBSESSED with winning these stupid Godlympics. It's all he thinks about! He's got Coach Trapezius training us, like, a gazillion hours a day.

Dad even brought in a guest coach—this Greek dude named Atlas. Oh, and here's what Atlas calls "coaching":

Atlas says he's taking the punishment your dad gave to him and passing it on to us. So now everyone here is barking mad at your dad, too!

Speaking of barking, did I tell you I have a dog? If I didn't, it's because I'm a little embarrassed. Her name is Cerbutterus. We named her that because she's got three butts! I know, I know—pretty weird, right? Well, get this: my dad is using my brother and my dog in a Godlympics commercial!

Doody Duffel: The official poop bag of the Godlympic Games!

Okay, I gotta go train—AGAIN! Hope I see you at the games . . . if I'm still alive!

Your friend,

Oddpollo

P.S. Between you and me, I kind of wish I were Greek right now!

CHAPTER 21

Whoa—there's so much to take in here!

I have a new friend!

Oddpollo has a dog just like mine!

We're all just pawns in our fathers' game of life!

There's not much we can do about it, though. When you're a kid, sometimes you just have to go along with what adults say—even when it doesn't make sense!

Speaking of not making sense, the grown-ups announce after practice the next day that the Godlympics are not going to take place at the school, like we thought. Instead, they're going to be held at the Olympia Stadium! That's the largest stadium in all Olympus!

"Isn't that a little much?" I ask Coach Gluteus Maximus. "These are *middle school games.*"

"You don't get it, son," replies Coach. "Two days from now, thousands of gung-ho Greeks and rabid Romans are going to be watching you. This is the biggest thing since the Trojan War!"

"You're darn tootin'!" adds Ms. Meticulous.

TOOOOOOOOOOOOT!!!! trumpets Gaseous. "I'm nervous just thinking about it!"

"Ugh," grunts Heracles. "Heracles not like being center of attention."

Even Adonis—who NEVER misses a chance to show off—seems uncertain. "Is that really necessary?" he asks.

"NECESSARY???" thunders Nike. "You bet it's

necessary! This is your chance to go out and show the world how to . . . let me hear you . . . !"

"Just Do It™," we all mumble halfheartedly.

"Correct!" shouts Principal Deadipus from his perch up in the stands. "You'll show my brother—I mean, you'll show the Romans what you're made of, if it's the last thing you do!!!"

The last thing we do? I can think of way better last things than that!

"Besides," continues Deadipus, "even if we wanted to use our school for the Godlympics, we cannot. At this very moment, it is being transformed into the Godlympic Village."

"What's the Godlympic Village?" I ask.

"Your father didn't tell you?" replies Deadipus. "Starting tomorrow, you are all moving in there for the games."

"We have to live at *school*?" gasps Gaseous.

"It's a dream come true!" cries Mathena.

"More like a nightmare!" snarls Puneous.

"And we all have to live . . . *together*?" asks Aphrodite, looking like she's smelling something bad. "Gods and . . . *Odds*?"

"And Romans," replies Principal Deadipus. "By order of Zeus and Jupiter."

"Is id so both sides of Olympus can exemplify de Godlympic spirid and lib togedder in peace and harbony?" asks Germes.

"Uh, no," says Deadipus. "I think it's so nobody can cheat."

CHAPTER 22

"I can't believe I have to leave home for these dumb Godlympics," pouts Gaseous as we stagger home after another grueling day. "I'll miss the smell of my room."

I don't know what Gaseous is talking about—because I've never actually smelled his room.

I'm about to make a crack about Gaseous's stench when I smell something HORRIBLE coming from my house. Oh, no. Tell me this isn't happening. No no no no no no no. It can't be! Gaseous and I take one more whiff. It is.

"LUTEFISK!!!" we howl together.

Lutefisk is, by far, my mother's *nastiest* Norwegian dish—and that's saying something. There are no words for lutefisk. Revolting? Repulsive? Foul? Vile? Horrid? That's being kind to lutefisk!

HOW TO MAKE
LUTEFISK

1. Take some codfish. Dry it.

2. Soak it in cold water for five days.

3. Then soak it in lye for two days. LYE! It's kinda like soap...BUT EVEN MORE POISONOUS!

4. Then soak for another week so it has the consistency of JELL-O. HELL-O! Fish should NEVER have the consistency of JELL-O!

And that's how you make lutefisk.

"G2G, dude!" yelps Gaseous, his eyes watering. "And BTW, I know you were about to say something about my room! Trust me, this is waaaaaay worse!"

Gaseous runs as fast as his legs will carry him. Meanwhile, my legs are wobbling as I walk in my front door.

"BOB?" I say. (That's "MOM?" when you're holding your nose.)

"Hallo, elskling!" calls Mom from the kitchen. "I made lutefisk for dinner!"

"You don'd say," I mutter.

"Better hurry," she says, "or your father and brother will eat it all!"

Nose burning and knees buckling, I lurch into the dining room to find Dad and Adonis scarfing down lutefisk like a couple of hungry narwhals.

"I LOOOOOOOVE LUTEFISK!!!" roars Adonis.

"Even though I'm against your father's Godlympic Village idea, I thought I'd make you boys a special last supper," says Mom. "You won't have my cooking for a few days, you know!"

Hey, hey—the Godlympic Village is looking better and better!

"The village is an essential part of the Godlympics experience, my dear," says Dad.

"So nobody can cheat?" I ask.

"No—for spying on the enemy!"

"You want your sons to spy on their opponents?" cries Mom. "Fy flate!"

"Fy yourself!" replies Dad. "Every little edge counts! This is war!"

"We don't need an edge, Dad," says Adonis. "We can beat the Romans on our own! We're the Greek Gods!"

"I can't take any chances, son. I have to beat Jupiter!"

"*You* have to beat Jupiter?" asks Mom.

"You know what I mean!" grumbles Dad. "We have to win . . . so you boys do what I tell you!"

Hmmm. The lutefisk isn't the only thing that stinks around here!

CHAPTER 23

The next morning, Adonis and I pack our bags for the Godlympic Village. Well, I might be leaving home, but there's no way I'm leaving my best buddy behind!

"Have fun, gutter!" Mom says to us.

"Fun?" scoffs Dad. "They're not going for fun—they're going to win!"

"You and your winning!" she snaps. "Det er helt hull i hodet!"

(I agree with Mom: that *is* completely hole in the head!)

"You are about to embark on a grand and glorious quest, Adonis," says Dad. "Not only will you represent Greek Mount Olympus, you'll stand for something far more important: ME. Make Daddy proud."

"I'll do my best, Great Father," replies Adonis.

"Do *more* than your best."

"Yes, sir."

"What about me, Dad?" I ask.

"Uhhh," ponders Dad. "Try not to get in the way, Oddonis."

My dad always knows exactly what to say, doesn't he? With those inspiring words of encouragement, Adonis and I head off to the Godlympic Village. (As usual, Adonis makes me follow five steps behind him—Gods forbid his friends see us walking together!) Neither of us is expecting much, but when we get to school, we don't even recognize it!

"Zeupiter?" we both say out loud.

Adonis and I follow the signs for Godlympians.
I have to admit, it's kind of cool! Whoever thought
I'd be a Godlympian? The only thing I've ever been
good at isn't very sporty. . . .

But check me out! I'm a world-class athlete now!

When we reach the gym, we find the floor lined with cots. I'm about to drop my bag next to one of them when Coach Gluteus Maximus stops me.

"Sorry, Oddonis, but these cots are for Godlympians only," he says.

"I *am* a Godlympian," I protest.

"Well, sort of," says the coach. "You're an assistant Godlympian."

"An assistant Godlympian?" I ask. "What does that mean?"

"It means you bring snacks to the Godlympians."

AGAIN WITH THE SNACKS!!!

"But I've been training for weeks!"

"Yes, you have," replies Coach. "And now you'll be able to deliver those snacks in no time!"

"You mean to tell me I pushed a boulder up a hill every day for *snack duty*?"

"Pretty much," Coach says. "Exciting, isn't it?"

"Not really!" I cry. "So where is my cot?"

"In the assistants' quarters," he says. "Right over there."

CHAPTER 24

"But that's . . . that's . . . that's . . . a *bathroom*!" I exclaim.

"Well, it's your room now!" Coach laughs.

It's bad enough that I have to be a snack carrier for the games—it's a whole other level of bad that I have to sleep in a *bathroom*! I guess I should be thankful we're not sleeping in the *girls'* bathroom! I've never set foot in a girls' bathroom in my entire life! Okay, maybe with my mom, but I've pretty much blocked that out.

Trianus pushes the door open ahead of me. Immediately, I'm welcomed by a familiar sound. . . .

PFFFFFFFFFFTTTTTTTTTTTTTTTTTTTTTTT!!!

And smell.

"Dis is fun!" snuffles Germes from inside a garbage can. "De bathroob is my *favorid* roob!"

Trianus is drawn to Germes like a fly on . . . something else you find in a bathroom. He will not stop smelling and licking him! No, Trianus, no! Don't do it! You've got so much to live for!

Thankfully, Trianus's sniff-fest is interrupted when a loud *"BUURRRRRRRRPPPPPPPPPPPPPPPP PPPPPPPPPPPPPPPPPPPPP!!!"* actually blows open the bathroom door! And there, standing in the door-way, are Belchous and Oddpollo . . . and Oddpollo's dog, Cerbutterus! As soon as Trianus sees her, he forgets all about Germes.

"'Scuse the burp," says Belchous. "Bumpy ride."

"Breathtaking, bro!" admires Gaseous.

"When did you guys get here?" I ask.

"A few minutes ago," replies Oddpollo. "And guess what? We just found out we're going to be schlepping snacks for the games."

"Us too," I groan.

"Hey, at least we get to sleep in a bathroom!" Puneous adds snarkily.

"Dat's de silber liding!" gushes Germes.

"You think this is bad?" says Oddpollo. "The girls have to sleep in the janitor's closet!"

"Oh, this I gotta see!" says Gaseous.

We run to Ajax the janitor's closet and knock on the door.

"WHO'S THAT???" screams a girl's voice. "ARE YOU A BURGLAR? A GHOST? WHAT DO YOU WANT FROM US, FOUL DEMON???"

"Calm down, Minervous," we say. "It's just us."

Slowly, the girls open the door. OMG—what a DUMP.

"When I dreamed of living at school," Mathena says with a sigh, "this is NOT what I had in mind!"

"I think id's nice," argues Bacteria. "Very hobey."

"Seems kind of dark to me," says Heightania.

"I don't like the dark!" sputters Minervous. "And I'm not crazy about the light, either!"

"Look, you guys," I say, "I'll admit, this is a pretty crummy situation—"

"But at least we're all in it together," says Oddpollo.

"Oh yeah?" clucks Mathena. "Tell that to our parents! They sure don't see it that way!"

"I'm afraid Mathena's right," I confess to the Romans. "You're not gonna believe this, but my dad actually ordered me to spy on all of you."

"Oh, I believe it," Oddpollo replies. "Because my dad told me to do the exact same thing!"

"So did mine," adds Mathena.

"MINE TOO!" wails Minervous. "It made me so tense!"

"Did *everyone's* parents tell them to spy?" I ask. "Raise your hands."

"Grown-ups," grumbles Puneous. "What babies!"

CHAPTER 25

Almost on cue, two huge *TWEEEEEEEEEEEEEETS!* ring out.

"Sounds like a real tweetstorm out there," Belchous says with a chuckle.

"Let's go," Gaseous replies with a grin. "But beware, Belchous—I'm watching you!"

We march back into the gym together and are met by some grim grown-up glares.

"Greeks on this side, Romans over there!" barks Coach Gluteus Maximus.

"Romans on this side, Greeks over there!" yelps Coach Trapezius.

"Welcome to Zeupiter Godlympic Village," Principal Deadipus says to us.

"Sponsored by Toyotus," Fredipus adds.

"Your last practice will commence after my remarks," announces Deadipus.

"*Our* remarks," snipes Fredipus. "After which you will report to the dining hall for a healthy, nutritious dinner—"

"Courtesy of Fryonysus," interrupts Deadipus, "official caterer of the Godlympic Games—"

"And tomorrow morning," interrupts Fredipus, "you will be issued your special uniforms for the opening ceremonies—

"Made by Mathena's mother, Athena," interrupts Deadipus, "official *Greek* Goddess of weaving—

"And UnderArmous," interrupts Fredipus, "official *Roman* clothing supplier."

"THATISALL!" they shriek, trying to outfast the other. "DISMISSED!"

TWEEEEEEEEEEEEEEEEEEEEEEEEEEEEEEEEET! TWEEEEEEEEEEEEEEEEEEEEEEEEEEEEEEEEET!

"Greeks out this door, Romans out the other!" screams Coach Gluteus Maximus.

"Romans out this door, Greeks out the other!" shouts Coach Trapezius.

"They should all take a major chill pill," whispers Gaseous.

"And stop trying to compete with each other," mutters Belchous. "Because they're *equally uncool*!"

We file out for our final pre-Godlympics workout. I have no idea why the Odds have to participate in this ridiculous charade, given our exalted SNACK duties, but we do. The coaches really let us have it, too. It's like they all want to one-up each other by seeing how much they can make US do! By the time dinner rolls around, our tanks are pretty much empty.

That night, Oddpollo and I have the same strange dream. We dream that the two of us win the God-lympics *together*. And we're getting kissed all over our faces!

In the morning, it's just like being at home . . . in a bad way.

"RISE AND SHINE, GREEKS!" crows Coach Gluteus Maximus.

"UP AND AT 'EM, ROMANS!" squawks Coach Trapezius.

"Hey," I yawn, "it's Godlympics Day, everybody."

The entire room is silent. Then, together, the Gods and Odds give a very sleepy, very sarcastic reply:

"Yippee."

CHAPTER 26

After a not-so-hearty breakfast (we just finish the food we were too tired to eat last night), we line up outside to receive our opening-ceremony uniforms. Or, I should say, the *Gods* line up. The Odds watch from afar, figuring that "assistant Godlympians" probably don't merit special outfits.

But when the uniforms are handed out, what we feel most is . . . relief! Because they . . . are . . . HID-EOUS! Get a load of these fashion statements!

"You've got to be kidding," gasps Aphrodite.

"*Who* made these again?" Adonis asks, barely concealing his rage and disgust.

"Mathena's mother," replies Principal Deadipus. "Athena."

"And UnderArmous," adds Fredipus.

"Were they sick when they made them?" asks Venus.

"Did you hear that?" says Fredipus. "Venus says these uniforms are sick!"

"Ooh! That's good, right?" asks Deadipus.

"*Really* good," Oddpollo and I whisper together.

"Let me get this straight," seethes Apollo. "You run us ragged, and then reward us with these clown costumes? Is this some kind of *joke*? You should give this weirdo wear to the Odd Gods!"

"Thanks," smirks Puneous, "but they definitely won't fit me."

"Or me!" echoes Heightania.

"Beauty is in the eye of the beholder, Apollo," replies Fredipus. "And don't you worry, Heightania and . . . umm . . . Teenytinyus—"

"Indeed!" exclaims Deadipus. "We've got uniforms for ALL the assistants!"

"Ruh-roh," mutters Oddpollo.

"Hey, they can't be any worse," I say.

"On second thought," I say with a sigh, "yes, they can."

"Ta-da! The official snacks of the Godlympic Games!" declares Fredipus.

"Seriously?" asks Puneous. "A pea?"

"Peas and carrots!" squeals Heightania. "Isn't that sweet, Puneous?"

"Adorable," grumbles Puneous.

"Beans, beans, the magical fruit!" bellows Belchous.

"The more you eat, the more you toot!" blares Gaseous.

"What if someone tries to take a bite out of me???" howls Minervous.

"I can't believe my mother did this to me," moans Mathena.

"Hey, at least your outfit makes sense," I say.

"Yeah," wails Oddpollo. "We're bloomin' onions, for cryin' out loud!"

Meanwhile, a powerful odor wafts out over the crowd.

Oddpollo and I check our underonions, but it's not us. We look around and quickly find the source of the stench: Germes and Bacteria. It's taken only a few minutes, but Germes's cheese costume is now green and moldy, and Bacteria's milk duds are gray and curdled!

"Ahhh," sniffles Germes. "Dat's more like id."

"M'm! M'm! Baaad!" bleats Bacteria.

"Just like these Godlympics," snarl Poseidon and Neptune.

"Baaad," grunt Heracles and Hercules.

"No more talk like that!" orders Coach Gluteus Maximus. "Line up next to your respective chariots! Greeks over here—Romans over there!"

"If you can't say something nice about the

Godlympics, don't say anything at all!" commands Coach Trapezius. "Romans over here—Greeks over there!"

As we joylessly take our places, it's plain to see our Godlympic spirits are way, way down. And our mood isn't helped when we get to our chariot. There, waiting for us, is our Debbius Downius driver, Phaethon.

"I'm Phaethon, your driver. My father is Helios, the Sun God. He granted me one wish, and I asked to drive his sun chariot across the sky. He said it would be too much for me. I said it wouldn't be, but it was, and I crashed. As punishment, I'm doomed to drive a school chariot for all eternity."

"¡Ay caramba!" snorts Sol, the Romans' driver. "This guy makes Hades look happy! Lighten up, fella!"

I wish we could tell all the grown-ups to lighten up. But as we board our chariots, it looks like that ship has sailed. Onward—and downward—we go!

CHAPTER 27

When we arrive at Olympia Stadium to get ready for the opening ceremonies, we can't believe our eyes. It's a mob scene.

The Greek fans are cheering us like mad, but the Roman fans are actually booing! They're even heckling us Odds—and we're just the snack squad!

"Booooo! I don't like peas!" screams some fan at Puneous.

"Eggs have high cholesterol!" yells another at Mathena.

"Onions make me cry!" a woman shouts at me.

When the Romans arrive, the same thing happens to them . . . in reverse. The Roman fans cheer, and the Greek fans boo! By the time we get past the crazed crowd and into the tunnel of the stadium, we're all a little spooked.

"Some Roman told me to jump in the lake," says Poseidon.

"Some Greek told me the last time he saw a mouth like mine, it had a hook in it," says Neptune.

"Heracles very scarred by that experience," murmurs Heracles.

"Hercules need to tell his therapist about this," mutters Hercules.

"Someone bumped into me . . . AND NOW MY APPLE IS BRUISED!" cries Minervous.

"Plus: scientific research shows that eggs cause levels of *good* cholesterol to rise!" claims Mathena.

"Okay, don't you guys see how screwy this is?" I ask.

"Yeah!" says Oddpollo. "Who are these games for anymore? Not us!"

"Don't listen to them, Greeks!" snaps Coach Gluteus Maximus. "You have a job to do! Zeus is counting on you!"

"Focus, Romans!" growls Coach Trapezius. "Jupiter needs you! And don't you forget it!"

"Come on, Adonis," I beg. "Even you can see this is messed up."

"Yeah, Apollo," pleads Oddpollo. "These are supposed to be games! Who needs this?"

Adonis and Apollo look at us. They look at the coaches. They scratch their heads, kick the ground with their sandals, and, finally, heave a huge sigh.

"You heard the coaches," Adonis says to us.

"Time to go to work," Apollo says to the Romans.

Trumpets blare a loud fanfare as we make our way through the tunnel and enter Olympia Stadium for the Parade of Athletes. Coach Gluteus Maximus leads the Greek Gods out first (us lowly snack servants make sure to walk ten steps behind). Coach Trapezius follows with the Roman Gods (and their equally humble refreshment roadies).

The stadium is packed to the rafters. The roar of the crowd is deafening. The whole building feels like it's shaking. The truth is, it's pretty awesome . . . and also a little frightening. But you know what's even more terrifying than the crowd? The faces of our guest instructors as we march by!

"Just Do It™!" thunders Nike.

"This means war!" howls Ms. Meticulous.

"Rock the house, Greeks!" shouts Sisyphus.

"The world's on your shoulders, Romans!" screams Atlas.

Well, I'm glad everyone has these games in perspective!

"Dude, this is wack!" hisses Gaseous (while hissing from another part of his body). "And speaking of wack, check out your dad!"

Sitting on four ginormous golden thrones in the center of the stadium are Mom and Dad, and Jupiter and Juno. I . . . I . . . I can't even.

"Dad!" Adonis and I gasp. "What are you wearing???"

"Pretty neat, huh?" whispers Dad. "Athena made

them! I called the bull, so Jupiter had to be the dopey oak tree!"

"Zip it, Zeus!" cries Jupiter. "Oak trees are strong!"

"Are not!" says Dad.

"Are too!" says Jupiter.

"Ti stille, Zeus!" snaps Mom. "Stop being so bull-headed!"

"Act your age, Jupiter," growls Juno, "or I'll give you a time-out!"

The two dads huff and puff, then stand up from their thrones. On cue, the formerly frenzied fans go completely silent. It's so quiet, you can hear a pin drop!

PFFFFFFFFFFFFFFFFFFFFFFFFFTTTTTTTT!!!

Okay, it's not a pin, but you get the idea!

CHAPTER 28

"Greetings, citizens of Mount Olympus!" booms Zeus. "Welcome to Nectarade Olympia Stadium!"

"For the first-ever middle school Godlympics!" roars Jupiter. "Brought to you by Bank of Olympus!"

"My fellow host and I need no introduction," says Zeus. "Well, I don't, at least. Everybody knows Zeus—"

"They know me too!" barks Jupiter. "I'm Jupiter! I'm very important!"

"Blah blah blah," grumbles Zeus. "Anyway, we are here to decide, once and for all, who is the best in all Olympus: the Greeks . . . or the Romans!"

"These Godlympians you see before you represent the greatest collection of middle school athletic talent the world has ever known!" exclaims Jupiter.

"And to them we say this," Zeus declares. "For these Godlympic Games, we hereby command you to remember—and follow—our Godlympic creed: The most important thing is not to PLAY, but to WIN!"

"Whatever it takes!" orders Jupiter. "WIN at all costs!"

"By hook or by crook!" demands Zeus. "WIN no matter what!"

"To the DEATH, if need be!" they thunder.

"To the *WHAT* did you say?" Freya and Juno gasp.

"You heard us! Just . . . WIIIIIIIIIIINNN!!!!"

And the crowd goes wild.

"Will the captains please come forward?" asks Zeus.

Adonis and Apollo take a step toward Zeus and

Jupiter. They look as shell-shocked as the rest of us.

"Do you, on behalf of your teammates, pledge to obey this Godlympic creed?" the Great Gods ask.

"Uhhh," stammers Adonis.

"Umm," splutters Apollo.

"Well???" the Great Gods sneer. "We're waiting!"

We're all waiting. Adonis and Apollo look at us, at Freya and Juno, and finally, at each other.

"No," says Apollo.

"No," says Adonis.

"NOOOOOOO?????" Zeus and Jupiter bellow.

All of us—Greeks and Romans, Gods and Odds—gather together and stand beside Adonis and Apollo.

"You heard them," I reply. "We say no."

And the crowd goes wilder.

CHAPTER 29

Zeus and Jupiter are beside themselves with anger.

(WEIRDEST. EXPRESSION. EVER.)

"WHAT DO YOU MEAN, NO???" they bluster.

"I mean we're not going to fight the Romans to the death," I reply. "That's just bonkers."

"In fact, we don't want to be a part of these Godlympics at all," adds Oddpollo. "This was supposed to be fun! And you grown-ups have sucked all the fun out . . . *again*!"

"But you can't say no!" Zeus screams. "We made these Godlympics for YOU!"

"Actually, Dad," I say, "I think you made them for *you*."

"You too, Papa," Oddpollo says to Jupiter. "All the Godlympic *stuff*—all the 'Brought to you by' this and 'Sponsored by' that and 'Official' whatever—that had nothing to do with us. That was all you guys!"

"Not to mention the constant coaching and nonstop workouts!" chimes in Adonis.

"And the endless interviews and commercials and promotions!" echoes Apollo.

"Heracles not a piece of meat!" grouses Heracles. "He not some trained seal!"

"Hercules not capitalist tool to be exploited!" grumbles Hercules. "He in it for love of game!"

"I beg your pardon," seethes Zeus, "but the

Godlympics are all about competition and sports-manship and *love*!"

"*Love???*" I fume. "You asked us to spy on them, Dad!"

"YOU DID???" Jupiter rages at Zeus. "HOW COULD YOU???"

"Oh, please, Papa—you asked us to spy, too!" Oddpollo scolds Jupiter.

"Face it, Dad," I say. "You just want to beat Jupiter."

"Ja—that's what you said, sukker," adds Mom.

"And you just want to beat Zeus, Papa," Oddpollo reminds Jupiter.

"Verissimo!" chirps Juno. "So true!"

"Yeah—and we don't want any part of it any-more!" Adonis declares.

"Right, you guys?" Apollo asks all of us.

"RIGHT!" we all roar.

"Well, we are having a Godlympics and that's final!" decrees Zeus.

"I'll second that, Zeus," agrees Jupiter. "If you children don't want to compete against each other, perhaps you'd like to compete against *us* instead!"

"Oh, baby!" howls Adonis. "Would we EVER!"

"Okay, boomers!" cries Apollo. "Bring it!"

"You're on!" thunders Zeus. "If we win, you kids go along with whatever Jupiter and I decide for Olympus—no questions asked, and no more back talk . . . EVER!"

"And if we win," I reply, "you stop this stupid feud with the Romans!"

"DONE!"

"Oh nei, oh nei!" moans Mom.

"Oh mio dei!" groans Juno.

"Tomorrow. Right back here," states Jupiter. "THE GODLYMPIC GAMES: KIDS VS. ADULTS!"

And the crowd goes wildest.

CHAPTER 30

Holy cow—it's like we signed a Declaration of Independence!

"WE'RE PLAYING THE GROWN-UPS!" we whoop.

Then reality sets in.

"We're playing the grown-ups," we whisper.

"Don't panic, you guys," I say.

"Are you sure?" asks Minervous. "It seems like a good time for panicking to me!"

"Oddonis is right," adds Mathena. "Let's approach this logically. First, we'll go back to the Godlympic Village and analyze our options. Then I'll make a spreadsheet. It'll be so fun!"

"Whoopee," sneers Puneous.

But when we get to the school chariots, the doors are closed!

"Hey, what gives, Sol?" asks Oddpollo. "Open the door!"

"No can do, kiddo!" replies Sol. "Boss's orders!"

"What about you, Phaethon?" I ask, knowing what I'm in for.

"I'm Phaethon, your driver. My father is Helios, the Sun God. He granted me one wish, and I asked to drive his sun chariot across the sky. He said it would be too much for me. I said it wouldn't be, but it was, and I crashed. As punishment, I'm doomed to drive a school chariot for all eternity. Except for today. Zeus gave me the rest of the day off, so I'm going to do something fun. I am going to stand in line at the post office!"

"Then how are we supposed to get back to the Godlympic Village?" wails Adonis. "That's like ten miles from here!"

"I know how you can get there," says Sol.

"How?" asks Apollo.

Hmmm. Very funny, Sol!

By the time we stumble into the village, it's dark and we're starving. But when we get in line for food at the cafeteria, we're met by a frightfully forlorn Fryonysus.

"Sorry, chums, but there's no chow!" apologizes Fryonysus. "The grown-ups took it all away!"

"NO FOOD???" howls Heracles. "Now you found Heracles's Achilles heel!"

"Food equal comfort to Hercules," admits Hercules. "And Hercules feeling very uncomfortable right now!!!"

"I'm so sorry." Fryonysus sighs. "I wish I could help."

"What the heck are we supposed to eat?" asks Belchous. "I can't burp on an empty stomach!"

"I've got a serious gas shortage here!" moans Gaseous. "I need to feed my furnace!"

"I'LL STARVE!!!" cries Minervous.

Suddenly the cafeteria door bursts open. Mamma Mia! It's Mom and Juno!

"Don't you worry, bambini!" trills Juno. "Mamma Juno and Mamma Freya are here to save the day!"

"Yumpin' yimini—you betcha!" cries Mom. "And have we got a treat for you! We made . . . LUTE-FISK!!!"

"I was going to make pizza, or spaghetti and meatballs, or maybe a lasagna," says Juno. "But Freya, she insisted! She says her boys LOVE their lutefisk!"

I thought there might be something fishy about these Godlympics. Now I know there is!

CHAPTER 31

After the moms leave, there's a definite air of sadness in the cafeteria. And it's not just the leftover lutefisk!

"What a horrible way to treat a fish," moans Neptune.

"Forget the fish," snarls Apollo. "What a horrible way for the grown-ups to treat us!"

"They take food!" cries Heracles. "It almost cruel!"

"They messing with our minds!" wails Hercules.

"Maybe we bit off more than we can chew," says Adonis. "I mean, they've got all the power, and we've got—"

"A whole lotta lutefisk." Poseidon sighs.

"Does that mean we're quitting?" asks Aphrodite excitedly.

"Oh, thank Gods," responds Venus. "I could really use a spa day."

"Quitting?" Puneous squawks. "Spa day? Are you serious? Who are you guys?"

"Puneous is right," adds Heightania. "You're Gods! Stand tall!"

"Easy for you to say, Ella Vator," replies Adonis. "You don't have to compete against the grown-ups!"

Hmmm.

"By George, that's it!" I declare.

"Who's George?" asks Adonis.

"Nobody," I reply.

"Then why'd you say 'By George'? Is George a God?"

"No."

"Is George an Odd God?"

"No."

"Then what does George have to do with this?"

"Nothing!" I shout. "It's an expression!"

"Well, it's a pretty silly expression, if you ask me," says Adonis. "And I'll bet you George would agree."

"Maybe we should ask George what he thinks," suggests Apollo.

"FORGET ABOUT GEORGE!" I holler.

"Can George help us win the Godlympics?" asks Gaseous.

"NO!!!" I yelp. "But if you hear me out, I think I know who can."

"That's great!" says Belchous. "Maybe we should wait a bit, though."

"Why should we wait?" I ask.

"Well, I'm sure George would like to hear too!"

"Look, I know where you're coming from," I say to the Gods. "I've been there. You're thinking there's no way you can win against the grown-ups. And it's true—you might not be able to beat them by yourselves. But you're not alone. You've got US!"

"Oddonis is right!" agrees Oddpollo. "We've got some mad odd skills. And we trained just as hard as you guys did, so we're in surprisingly good shape!"

"He's got a poind," seconds Bacteria. "Germes—I'b been beaning to tell you how brawdy you look!"

"Plus," I add, "the grown-ups won't work together. They don't even like each other! But we do!"

"See what I mean?" I proclaim to the Gods. "We can do this!"

"So what are *we* supposed to do?" asks Adonis.

"Nothing! Just kick back and leave everything to us!" Then I turn and roar as loudly as I can: "ODD GODS! ASSEMBLLLLLLLLLLLLE!!!"

"We're right here," says Mathena. "We've been here literally the entire time you have."

"Sorry—I guess I got carried away."

"What exactly do you want from us?" Mathena asks.

"Follow me, and you'll see!" I reply.

BRRRRRAAAAAAAAACKK!!! booms Gaseous. "This is so exciting! Ooh—and if you tell me what he looks like, I'll go get George, too!"

CHAPTER 32

While the Gods put their feet up, the Odd Gods get down to work.

In the morning, the Gods are exhilarated, and the Odds are exhausted . . . but determined. We're helped out by an anonymous PANCAKE delivery— though we all know who's responsible: Fryonysus! What a pal! We need every bite of those flapjacks, too, because the grown-ups block our chariots again and we have to walk all the way *back* to Olympia Stadium! To lift our spirits while we walk, I come up with a rousing chant:

I DON'T KNOW BUT I'VE BEEN TOLD,

I DON'T KNOW BUT I'VE BEEN TOLD,

ALL OUR FOLKS ARE REALLY OLD!

ALL OUR FOLKS ARE REALLY OLD!

I DON'T KNOW BUT IT'S BEEN SAID,

I DON'T KNOW BUT IT'S BEEN SAID,

WHEN THEY FACE US THEY'LL

WET THE BED!

WHEN THEY FACE US THEY'LL WET THE BED!

SOUND OFF—ONE TWO!

SOUND OFF—THREE FOUR!

But Germes ends the chant when he sings, "FIVE SIX—I HAVE TICKS!"

The stands are filled when we arrive at the stadium, and we have to squeeze through the gauntlet of grumblers again.

"Booooo!!!!" they scream. "Youth is wasted on the young!"

"Children should respect their elders!"

"Onions still make me cry!"

ACK! Why did Oddpollo and I wear these onion costumes again???

Olympia Stadium is jammed, and when we march in, it gets so loud we can't even hear ourselves think! It feels like all of Olympus—Greek and Roman—is here. The adults take up most of the seats, but there's a very enthusiastic, very vocal bunch of little kids sitting in one corner of the stadium. And guess who's sitting with them? Mom and Juno! So cool! They've made some super signs, too!

The adults are not happy about the moms or the signs—especially my dad.

"Two can play at that game!" roars Zeus. He turns to his followers in the crowd and yells up to them, "All right, everyone! On the count of three, turn over the GO GROWN-UPS! cards you were given when you entered the stadium! One! Two! Three!"

I don't think this is what Dad had in mind.

"Come on!" Dad growls. "Really?!?"

"Forget about it, Zeus," Jupiter says. "Let's teach these whippersnappers a lesson they'll NEVER forget!"

"Right you are, Jupiter!" bellows Zeus. "But first we will light the Godlympic flame! Ladies and gentlemen, give it up for Hephaestus and Vulcan—Great Gods of fire!"

Hephaestus and Vulcan enter carrying torches. They stand next to a giant cauldron at the far end of the stadium.

"I hereby light the Godlympic flame, symbol of unity and goodwill!" announces Hephaestus.

"Excuse me, Hephaestus," Vulcan interrupts, "but *I* hereby light the Godlympic flame of unity and goodwill."

"I beg your pardon, Vulcan," sneers Hephaestus, "but I was here first, and *I* will light the flame of unity and goodwill!"

"Umm, I don't think so!" snaps Vulcan. "That flame of unity and goodwill is MINE!"

"IT'S MINE!"

"MINE!"

"MINE!"

Hephaestus and Vulcan are about to come to blows when, out of nowhere, Gaseous butts in!

"Out of the way, Mr. Unity and Mr. Goodwill!" my best bud thunders. "Gaseous is in the house!"

"Now that's how you light a Godlympic flame!" Gaseous yells. "Let's get it on, grown-ups!"

Oh, baby—we're all stoked now! Looks like Gaseous lit a fire under us, too!

CHAPTER 33

EVENT ONE:
THE LONG JUMP

The grown-ups trot out their contestant for the first event: Hermes.

"Dat's my fodder!" squeals Germes. "How aboud a hug, Dada?"

"Umm . . . maybe later, son," replics Hermes. "After Dada's donc jumping!"

"Bud I wand a hug dow!" Germes pouts. "Come od, Dada!"

"Oh, all right." Hermes sighs. "But just a quick one, okay?"

I'm wondering why Hermes is so hesitant, until I see him *after* the hug.

That is one sick power Germes has—and I mean *sick*! Unfortunately, it doesn't stop Hermes from landing a monster long jump. He and his winged sandals fly through the air with the greatest of ease and touch down in a sand pit almost fifty yards away!

"Now that's what I call a LONG JUMP!" roars Zeus. And the crowd roars right along with him.

Hermes doesn't seem that happy, though. He struggles to his feet and staggers out of the pit, mumbling, "Ohhhh . . . why did I give him a hug? Ohhhhh . . ."

It was a really long long jump, but thanks to Germes's toxic touch, it wasn't Hermes's *longest*. Unfortunately, that doesn't seem to mean much to our contestant—Adonis.

"How the Hades am I supposed to jump that far?" he complains. "I don't have winged sandals!"

"Don't worry," I whisper to him. "You've got a secret weapon!"

"I hate to break it to you, Oddy," he replies, "but my fabulous looks and charming personality aren't going to help my jumping!"

Oh, brother.

"Trust me," I say. "We've got this."

172

Adonis steps to the line, and just as he rears back to jump . . .

"WAIT!" bellow Gaseous and Belchous. The two of them stand right behind Adonis—Belchous facing toward him, and Gaseous facing *away* from him . . . if you know what I mean.

"Ready!" they yell.

"WHAT'S GOING ON HERE?" cries Adonis.

"You're gonna need a boost!" they reply. "Now . . . JUMP!"

Adonis jumps—and Gaseous and Belchous boost!

Adonis takes off like he's been shot from a cannon—which hasn't even been invented yet! He hurtles through the air, finally touching down in the sand more than fifty yards *past* Hermes's mark! The grown-ups are silenced—and the kids go ballistic!

"That's one small burp and fart for kids . . . ," I say.

"One giant leap for kidkind!" says Oddpollo.

Adonis exits the sand pit, swaggers past Zeus and Jupiter, and boasts, "Hey, dads—*that's* what you call a long jump!" Then he turns to me and gloats, "I don't know what you were so anxious about. I had it the whole time!"

CHAPTER 34

EVENT TWO: THE DISCUS

Now that we got the "jump" on the grown-ups in Event One, it feels like the wind is at our backs. (Of course, that could just be Belchous's belches and Gaseous's gas at our backs!) But we really like our chances in the discus event, because our contestants are Heracles and Hercules! We're so confident that our only problem might be that we're *too* confident—or, at least, *some* of us are.

"We are going to DEMOLISH the grown-ups!" brags my brother.

"What can we do to help?" I ask Adonis. "The Odd Gods are ready, willing, and able!"

"Please," Adonis replies, "you might be ready and willing, but you're not exactly able."

"Are you sure we can't lend a hand or . . . something else?" asks Gaseous. "I always keep a spare in my reserve tank, if you get my drifffffffffffftttttttttt."

"I get it, and . . . gross."

"I'm ready too," says Belchous. "Just shake me well before using!"

"Thanks but no thanks, Bubblous," replies Apollo. "Hercules and Heracles will be just fine on their own."

"Are you absolutely, positively, one hundred percent certain about that?" asks Mathena. "I mean, they're not the sharpest crayons in the box."

"Yeah, they're a few sandwiches short of a picnic," adds Minervous.

"They're not doing geometry, Nerdthena," says Adonis. "They're throwing plates!"

"Yeah, it's brawn, not brains!" Apollo chides Minervous. "Stop your worrying!"

Heracles and Hercules step to the line. They stand side by side, Heracles cradling his discus in his right hand and Hercules holding his in his left. They turn to Adonis and Apollo and ask, "What we do with this thing again?"

"Oh. My. Gods," says Adonis. "What do you think you do, numbskulls?"

"Throw it, you dopes!" shouts Apollo. "THROW IT!!!"

Heracles and Hercules rock back and forth, back and forth, synchronizing their movements—and then, in perfect harmony, they hop from one foot to another, twirl like ballerinas, and . . . CRASH RIGHT INTO EACH OTHER!

The discuses tumble out of their hands and land at their feet. #FAIL.

"WHOAAAAAAAAA!!!" snorts Zeus. "DID YOU SEE THAT???"

"DID I EVER!!!" howls Jupiter. "THEY'RE A SMASH HIT!!!"

"Nononononononononononono!" cries Minervous.

"It's a good thing they didn't need any help," Mathena mutters sarcastically.

"And now for *our* contestants," say Zeus and Jupiter. "Deadipus and Fredipus, would you do the honors?"

"With pleasure, sires," reply Deadipus and Fredipus. The two old bags of bones walk past our comatose combatants, pick up the discuses, and drop them a foot in front of the line.

"Mic drop!" say Deadipus and Fredipus.

So cold! And so weird—because the mic drop hasn't been invented yet, either!

CHAPTER 35

**EVENT THREE:
THE FOOT RACE**

We need to get our mojo back ASAP! After our discus disaster, even the snotty Gods can see that we're going to need all the help we can get—and we Odds are psyched to pitch in. But our enthusiasm is dampened when we see who's running the footrace for the grown-ups.

"JustDoIt™JustDoIt™JustDoIt™JustDoIt™-JustDoIt™JustDoIt™!" Nike mumbles to herself. Scary! But we've got someone even scarier on our side!

Officially speaking, Aphrodite and Venus are running the footrace for us. But Oddpollo and I tell Minervous to line up next to Nike and have a little prerace chat with her.

"Me? Talk to Nike?" Minervous asks nervously. "What should I talk to her about?"

"Anything that comes to mind," I reply.

"And we mean a . . . ny . . . thi . . . ng," adds Oddpollo.

"Okaaaaaay," she replies anxiously. "I just hope I don't get tongue-tied. Or have dry mouth. Or throw up!"

Nike is already at the starting line—head down, crouched in position, stretching her calves. Minervous plants herself next to Nike . . . and lets her freak flag fly!

"Hi, Nike," squeaks Minervous.

"Just Do It™," whispers Nike.

"I'm so scared to be talking to you," Minervous continues. "I mean, you're a . . . a . . . *Goddess*! You're a star and I'm nobody! I'm shaking like a leaf here! I really have to pee, too. Do you ever have to pee when you get nervous?"

"No," grunts Nike, shifting around in her stance.

"Well, I do," says Minervous. "Then I get nervous I won't be able to find a bathroom and that makes me have to pee even more! So I start trying to hold it in—oh, and that makes it WAY worse! I'm holding the pee in and looking around for a bathroom and there isn't one so I start thinking OMG what do I do if I can't find a bathroom in time? Where will I go? What will happen? You know what I mean?"

"Can you stand somewhere else, please?" Nike replies through gritted teeth.

"Runners, take your places!" shouts Coach Gluteus Maximus.

"So now it's getting really hard to hold it in!" says Minervous. "And to make matters worse, I start hearing water running all over the place, too! It's like I'm surrounded—by WATER! Isn't that crazy???"

"I am getting DESPERATE now! I'm *totally* panicking. I'm frantically searching for somewhere to go. But where? WHERE? Behind that statue over there? Next to that hot-dog cart? Or, Gods forbid, underneath the STANDS? But what if someone SEES ME? How embarrassing will that be? I've got no choice, though! When you gotta go, you gotta go, right?"

"*Please . . . leave,*" groans Nike, bobbing up and down in her stance.

"On your mark!" cries Coach Trapezius.

"And then it hits me," gasps Minervous. "I'M NOT GOING TO MAKE IT! I am going to pee RIGHT HERE!"

"Don't Do It™! Don't Do It™! Don't Do It™!" moans Nike.

"Get set!" screams Coach Gluteus Maximus.

"AND EVERYONE IN THE WHOLE WIDE WORLD IS GOING TO WATCH ME DO IT!" wails Minervous. "Now I'm sweating buckets! My head is spinning! My stomach is in knots! I can't take it anymore! HELP! I NEED RELIEF! The floodgates open, and—"

"GO!!!" yell the coaches.

"AAAHHHHHHH!" shrieks Nike. "I HAVE TO PEEEEEEEEEEEEEEEEEEEEEEEEEEEEEE!!!!"

The crowd is peetrified . . . I mean, petrified.

Meanwhile, Aphrodite and Venus are still standing at the starting line, stunned, startled, and stupefied.

"Should we go?" they ask.

"Yes—go!" we shout.

"But don't go like Nike did!" warns Gaseous. "Just . . . you know . . . GO!"

"And try not to fall!" adds Minervous.

Heeding Minervous's warning, Aphrodite and Venus jog carefully down the track. The kids in the crowd are cheering, and when it becomes clear that Nike is not coming back from her wee-wee break, Aphrodite and Venus pick up their pace and start running freely . . . confidently . . . even joyfully! They cross the finish line, and our whole team rushes to congratulate them. But Oddpollo and I stay back to salute our real hero.

"Gee, thanks, you guys," says Minervous. "Now, can you do *me* a favor?"

"Name it," we reply.

"TELL ME WHERE THE BATHROOM IS!!!"

CHAPTER 36

EVENT FOUR:
THE JAVELIN

The adults aren't messing around with Event Four. It's their last chance to tie the score, so they send out Diana, the Roman hunting goddess, to throw the javelin for them. Apollo and Oddpollo can't believe their eyes . . . because Diana is their *sister*!

"What the hunt, Di?" Apollo asks Diana.

"Yeah, sis," adds Oddpollo, "why are you helping the grown-ups?"

"Dad said he'd give me my own forest," replies Diana. "Do *you* have a forest you can give me, Oddpollo?"

"No, but—"

"How about you, Apollo? Got any forests lying around that you wanna fork over?"

"No, but—"

"Then step aside while I crush this javelin."

Boy, is she strict! Diana steps up to the line, javelin in tow—but instead of throwing it, she reaches over her shoulder and pulls out a large hunting bow.

"Oh, no," groans Oddpollo. "She's got the bow."

"Wait—is that even legal?" I ask. "Aren't you supposed to *throw* a javelin?"

"We say it's legal!" trumpet Zeus and Jupiter. "Judges, what do you say?"

"Oh, yes," parrot Deadipus and Fredipus. "One hundred percent!"

"They're the judges?" gripes Puneous. "That's real fair!"

"Sour grapes make the best *whine*, Puneous," sneers Deadipus.

"Hear, hear!" agrees Fredipus. "However Diana propels her javelin forward is fine with us!"

"Wise decision!" hoots Jupiter. "Let 'er rip, Diana!"

Diana nestles the javelin in the crook of her bow, pulls back the string, and launches it into the air. It is high . . . it is far . . . it is . . . GONE! More than a hundred yards, to be precise!

"Whoaaaaaaa," the crowd ooohhhs.

"Yiiiiiiiiikes," we all arrgggghhhhh. This is not good.

"No worries, you guys," Oddpollo cheers. "My sister isn't the only one who can use a bow! It's one of my brother Apollo's symbols!"

But Apollo just stands there with his eyes glazed, looking white as a toga.

"I'm good with a lyre," he whispers to Oddpollo, "but I'd be a liar if I said I was as good as Diana with a bow. She's much better than me! I'm going to need a lot of help!"

"Relax, bro," Oddpollo assures Apollo. "Just do your thing, and we'll do the rest." Then Oddpollo claps his hands and calls out, "READY, ODDS? ASSUME YOUR POSITIONS!"

The Odd Gods move like a well-oiled machine. Mathena and Puneous park themselves on either side of Apollo, and Mathena takes a funny-looking gadget out of her pocket.

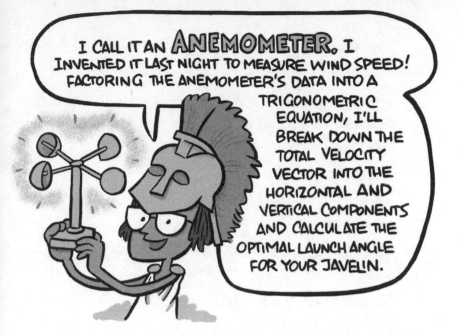

"Okaaaay," answers Apollo. He grabs his bow, loads the javelin into place, and mutters, "Here goes nothing!"

"WAIT!" barks Puneous. "Hold your horses, bub!"

Puneous leaps onto the javelin. Then he shinnies his way up to the middle of it and lies down!

"This thing won't fly itself, y'know!" he roars. "I mean, it will—technically speaking, that is—but you get the picture!"

"Not really," replies Apollo.

"Whatever!" shouts Puneous. "LET'S DO THIS!"

"400 fpm!" cries Mathena.

"Check!" replies Puneous.

"vx 13.5 m/s! vy 6.8 m/s!"

"Check! Check!"

"θ = tan (14.6 m/s/8.62 m/s)!"

"Enough!"

"Roger that!" yells Mathena. "All yours, Apollo! Ready! Aim! Fire!"

The javelin rockets out of Apollo's bow. Thanks to Mathena's anemenomenahomanahomana . . . thingy, it arcs higher and higher in the air, like a majestic bird in flight. The crowd is mesmerized.

Now Puneous takes over. He leans this way and that, adjusting to the wind, using aerodynamics to steer the soaring stick forward. Puneous is flying faster than a speeding bullet. (One more thing that hasn't been invented yet!)

"Oh, boy, is this great!" I exclaim.

Then we hear a tiny, angry "HELLLLLLLLLLLPPPP!" and realize we forgot about one thing: Puneous's exit strategy!

"Oh, boy, is this awful!" I exclaim.

"STOP THIS CRAZY THING!!!!!" screams Puneous.

"Don't worry, little buddy!" cries Heightania. "I'll save you!"

Heightania dives to the ground and stretches as far as she can—which is really, really far! She holds out her hands and calls to Puneous, "Jump off and I'll catch you!"

"YOU'D DO THAT FOR ME?" asks Puneous.

"Of course!" replies Heightania. "That's what friends are for!"

Adonis's javelin zooms another hundred yards past the spot where Diana's landed and plunges into the grass with a resounding *THWACK!!!*

"PHEW and WOOHOOOOO!!!" we shout.

"IN YOUR FACE, GROWN-UPS!" crows Puneous. "And three cheers for my friend Heightania! She's a tall drink of water!"

"Hurray for my friend Puneous!" hails Heightania. "He's a small miracle!"

"No fair! No fair!" scream Zeus and Jupiter. "You can't throw a javelin like that!"

"Judges?" I ask. "What do you say?"

"Umm . . . errr . . . uhhh," stammer Deadipus and Fredipus.

"Audience?" Mom and Juno ask the crowd. "You heard the judges before! What do *you* say?"

"However you propel your javelin forward is fine with us!" the crowd cheers.

"Wise decision!" hoot the moms. "Sorry, grown-ups—kids win!"

CHAPTER 37

"**B**ite i gresset, Zeus," Mom says to Dad. (That's Norwegian for "Bite the grass," but it really means, "Admit defeat.")

"NEVER!" thunders Zeus.

"Wake up and smell the nectar, Dad," says Adonis. "You're down 3–1. There's no way you can win!"

"Oh, yeah?" blurts out Zeus. "Then we'll bet even more!"

"Right!" chimes in Jupiter. "We'll double our wager! We'll triple it! We'll . . . we'll . . . whatever comes next it!"

"What exactly are you doubling?" asks Mathena. "Or tripling? Or QUADRUPLING? What are you going to add to the bet?"

"We'll . . . we'll . . . ," splutters Jupiter, "we'll let you kids run Olympus!"

"You'll *what*?" cries Apollo.

"Right!" says Zeus. "And we'll . . . we'll . . . we'll all be your servants for the rest of the year!"

"Servants!" hisses Adonis. "Sweeeeeeet!!!"

"And to show you all that I back up my words with actions," Dad continues, "*I* will represent the adults in this event."

"Ahem!" coughs Jupiter. "You mean *WE*."

"Very well," Zeus says begrudgingly. "The contest shall have *two* athletes per team. Why, we'll even let you kids choose the event! BUT . . ."

There's always a BUT, isn't there?

"You *must* pick a twosome that has not yet participated in these games."

"Okay with us!" replies Adonis.

"Who hasn't participated?" asks Apollo.

"Not okay with us!" says Adonis.

"What's the matter?" sneers Zeus. "Are you . . . *chicken?*"

Oh, no. More bawking.

"What do we do?" asks Apollo. "They're bawking us!"

"What is it with you guys and bawking?" howls Mathena. "Who cares? I *like* bawking! And I *love* chickens!"

"Yeah, we're ahead!" pleads Minervous. "Don't tempt fate!"

But we know the eternal unwritten rule: you can never back down from a bawk. Doesn't matter if you're Greek or Roman. It's basically illegal.

"Okay, Dad." Oddpollo and I sigh. "You're on."

CHAPTER 38

"**E**xcellent!" Zeus grins.

"I'm glad to see that our sons aren't chicken," adds Jupiter.

"On behalf of chickens everywhere, I object!" states Mathena, cradling a crestfallen Clucky in her arms.

"So, boys," Zeus says to Oddpollo and me, "do tell—what's it going to be? In what event . . . hee hee hee . . . are the four of us . . . haw haw haw . . . going to . . . *'compete'*?"

Dad does that air quotes thing with his fingers when he says "compete." So annoying! And, unfortunately, so true!

"We need to talk it over," Adonis replies.

"We'll be waiting." Dad smirks.

"While they do that," Mom and Juno bark at Dad and Jupiter, "*WE* need to talk something over with the two of you!"

Oh mamas—it looks like Mom and Juno mean business!

"Who are you supposed to be?" asks Dad.

"We're the kids' lawyers!" replies Mom.

"What's a *lawyer*?" Jupiter shudders. "It sounds dreadful!"

"We are here to make sure that you two don't cheat!" says Juno.

"Right!" adds Mom. "You may not use any of your powers in this event!"

"Whaaaaat?" ask the Great Gods.

"You heard us," snaps Juno. "You're going to play fair and square. That means no lightning bolts—"

"No lightning bolts!" shouts Zeus.

"—no eagles, and no rainstorms of any kind!"

"Not even a little sprinkle?" asks Jupiter.

"Niente!" growls Juno. "Nothing!"

"Now, sign these documents we've drawn up," orders Mom. "And tell us where we can bill you."

While the moms deal with the dads, the kids deal with an even bigger issue: Oddpollo and I are both terrible at sports!

"Come on—there's gotta be something you guys can do!" wails Adonis. "Aren't you good at anything?"

Hmmm.

Nope.

"But Zeus and Jupiter can't use any of their powers!" says Apollo. "Mathena, doesn't that give us a chance?"

"Hypothetically yes, but the chances are slim," Mathena replies. "After factoring in age, height, weight, and body mass index, I calculate that even if the grown-ups are powerless we are still at a twenty-five percent disadvantage. That is the mathematical equivalent of Oddonis and Oddpollo having three legs and Zeus and Jupiter having four."

Hmmm again!

I don't know what that thing is over my head—but I do know that I have an idea!

"I've got it!" I say. "And it just might work!"

CHAPTER 39

FINAL EVENT:
THE THREE-LEGGED
RACE

"**Y**ou've got to be kidding me!" moans Zeus.

"This is the stupidest thing I've ever done!" groans Jupiter.

"Well, you said the kids could choose the event!" scold the moms.

"Ugh," grumble the dads. "Lawyers!"

I've only run a three-legged race once before, at a school picnic. I did surprisingly well—but that had more to do with my partner than with me!

"If we can't use our powers," Dad complains to Mom, "then they can't have help from their freaky little friends!"

"That means no belching, no tooting . . . and no math!" echoes Jupiter.

"Can'd I gib you a good lug handshake?" asks Germes.

"Back it up, Captain Contagious!" warns Zeus.

"Can't I mention how dangerous this event is, especially for someone your age?" asks Minervous. "I mean, the risk of hip fracture is . . ."

"Whoop whoop whoop!" hoots Jupiter, sticking his fingers in his ears.

"Fair enough," Mom states. "No one gets help of any kind. Understood?"

"Guess that means no gas power, Oddy," says Gaseous.

"Or God power," Adonis whispers in my ear. "It's all up to you, brother. You're on your own now."

"But I'm not on my own," I reply. "I've got my teammate right here!"

"Thanks, partner," says Oddpollo. "Let's take the cheese!"

We get in position. The coaches scream, "Ready! Set! GO!!!" and we're off! Well, at least Oddpollo and I are!

"I'm going first!" growls Zeus.

"No, *I'm* going first!" snarls Jupiter.

"I am King of the Gods, and I decide who will go first!"

"Helloooo! I'm King of the Gods too!"

"ARE NOT!"

"ARE TOO!"

"You're ruining this whole thing, you big baby!" barks Zeus.

"I'm not the one who's ruining it—you are!" snaps Jupiter.

"AM NOT!"

"AM TOO!"

While the Titans are clashing, Oddpollo and I are matching each other's strides, step for step. Neither of us has EVER been fast on our own—but together, we're like a three-legged cheetah!

"This is so cool!" I shout to Oddpollo. "Look at us go!"

"It's amazing! I've never run this fast in my whole entire life!" Oddpollo yells back.

The crowd is going bananas. Half of them are cheering us on, while the other half is begging Zeus and Jupiter to TAKE ONE MEASLY STEP!

"STOP SQUABBLING!" they plead. "AND START SCURRYING!"

"OH, I WILL—as soon as HE gets out of my way!" cries Zeus.

"I'M not in YOUR way!" wails Jupiter. "YOU'RE in MY way!"

Think it can't get any better? Or worse? It can. Zeus and Jupiter start pushing and shoving . . . and then wrestle each other to the ground!

"What are they doing now???" I gasp.

"I don't know, but we better hurry!" replies Oddpollo.

We pick up our pace. We fly around the track, three-legging as one. The Kings of the Gods are still rolling around at the starting line when Oddpollo and I make it around to the finish! I gotta say . . . it's a little anticlimactic.

"Dad?" I say.

"Dad?" Oddpollo says.

"GET. OFF. OF. ME!" grunts Zeus.

"YOU. GET. OFF. OF. ME!" snorts Jupiter.

"DAD!!!!"

Zeus and Jupiter stop scuffling. Dazed, dusty, bruised, and battered, they look up. I almost feel sorry for them!

"Oh, hello, Oddy," Zeus replies.

"Hello, son," Jupiter says to Oddpollo. "Is it time to start the race?"

"Lyset er på, men ingen er hjemme," Mom says, sighing. (That's Norwegian for "The lights are on, but nobody's home.")

"Sorry, Dads," Oddpollo and I reply. "The race is over, and . . . OMG . . . WE WON!!!"

CHAPTER 40

Oddpollo and I get MOBBED by our teammates! Heracles and Hercules throw us high in the air and then wrap us up in a big, slightly scary bear hug.

"Heracles so happy, Heracles walking on air!" Heracles screams.

"Hercules feel very validated!" Hercules cries. "Hercules can't wait to journal about it!"

"Looks like I'll have to recalculate," Mathena says with a smile. "You beat the odds."

"Correction!" cackles Puneous. "They beat the Gods!"

"Correction," I reply. "We *all* did."

"That's right—we ALL did!" brags Adonis. "That includes me!"

"And me!" boasts Apollo.

Adonis and Apollo grab Oddpollo and me and pull us in close. Oh, no . . . are they going to slug us?

"Listen, you two," Adonis whispers. "Just so you know . . ."

"We couldn't have done this without you," whispers Apollo.

"And we'll both deny we ever said that," Adonis adds.

Wow! Oddpollo and I will take that over slugging any day!

The party's just getting started, as our fans join us on the field—led by our biggest fans of all: our moms! Let the squeeeeezing begin!

"I'm so proud of you, kjære!" beams Mom.

"So proud, topolino!" Juno tells Oddpollo.

"But I'm curious," says Mom. "Why did you choose a three-legged race?"

"Si," says Juno. "How did you know that would work?"

"It was easy," I reply. "I knew it required *team-work*."

BWOOOOOONKKK!/"*BURRRRRPPPPP!*"
Gaseous and Belchous fart-burp (furp?) together.

"Okay, not exactly what I had in mind," I say, "but you get the point. We've all learned how to cooperate, get along, and work together. It didn't matter if we were totally similar . . .

"Or totally different . . .

"We were a team. And the grown-ups . . . weren't."

"And we're not just a team," adds Oddpollo. "We're *friends*, too."

"Well, well, it seems you've taught us all a valuable lesson," says Mom. "Right, grown-ups?"

"Right," reply Coach Gluteus Maximus and Coach Trapezius.

"So right," reply Deadipus and Fredipus.

"Just Do It™," replies Nike.

Mom and Juno turn to Dad and Jupiter. "Well, boys?" they ask.

"Right," they whisper.

"So we can all hear you!"

"RIGHT!" the Great Gods thunder.

"That's better."

"So, your team won," Zeus says to us. "I guess that means you're in charge."

"Yes." Jupiter sighs. "It looks like you'll be running Mount Olympus now."

"We don't want to be in charge," I say. "And we don't want to run *anything*. We just want to be kids!"

"But . . . we do have some demands," states Oddpollo.

"What kind of demands?" ask Zeus and Jupiter.

"We don't want to be the grown-ups," Oddpollo says. "We want *you* to be the grown-ups!"

"*And* remember what's most important," I say. "Being together . . . and having fun!"

Total silence. Followed by TOTAL PANDAMO-NIUM!

Oops! Sorry! Spelled it wrong. I meant TOTAL PAND<u>E</u>MONIUM!!! The crowd goes crazy. The stadium is rocking! The grown-ups even surprise us with this!

"We hear you, children," Zeus and Jupiter say. "And we will try our best."

"Thanks, Dad," Oddpollo and I reply.

"No, boys, thank *you*," Jupiter says, "for giving us the chance to learn from our mistakes—and for letting us have our kingdoms back."

"No prob."

"Oh, and one more thing," Zeus laughs. "Thanks

for forgetting about that whole 'We'll be your servants for the rest of the year' thing. That was very nice of you."

Hmmm.

EPILOGUE

Hey, we're nice . . . but we're not *that* nice!